INDIAN SUMMER

TRACY RICHARDSON

LUMINIS BOOKS

LUMINIS BOOKS
Published by Luminis Books
13245 Blacktern Way, Carmel, Indiana, 46033, U.S.A.
Copyright © Tracy Richardson, 2010

Cover design and composition for *Indian Summer* by Vincent C.
Cannon.

ISBN-10: 1-935462-25-3

ISBN-13: 978-1-935462-25-5

Printed in the United States of America

10 9 8 7 6 5 4 3 2

For Chris, with you anything's possible.

And,

For Mom, your spirit lives on.

Praise for *Indian Summer:*

Indian Summer is a unique read middle school readers will relish.

—*Midwest Book Review*

I've been blessed in these past few weeks with young adult books that have taken me to places I have absolutely not wanted to come back from. This book will be one that will sit on my shelf for a very long time, and I will pass along to my daughter and to her daughter. I loved this book.

The writer really delved into all the areas of teenage angst. From the gut-wrenching scenes of peer pressure to the maximum, when poor Marcie has to find a way to fit into a world that she doesn't understand—and doesn't even like—to the effects that big business has on nature conservancy and preservation of the past—the author has found a way to focus on major issues in an absolutely fun and exciting way.

I look forward to reading a lot more in the future from this writer.

—*Amy Lignor, Bookpleasures*

Unlike many stories in this genre, Richardson presents conflicts and issues that are subtly shaded, with no clear good versus bad, right versus wrong. This real-world treatment of complex social and environmental issues places *Indian Summer* a notch above similar stories.

Richardson creates complex yet realistic relationships. *Indian Summer* is a thoughtfully-written story requiring the reader to consider a number of value judgments along the way. For the YA reader . . . an entertaining and informative read—thoughtfully-written adventure with a hint of magic.

—*Thomas E. Temple, Amazon Customer Review*

An enjoyable young adult tale that focuses on how a courageous but frightened tweener sees things in an adult world. Marcie is terrific . . . middle school fans will enjoy Marcie's charming Indian Summer.

—*Harriet Klausner, The Merry Genre Go Round Reviews*

The storyline [of *Indian Summer*] is calming, interesting, and intriguing . . . it also gives a feeling of suspense. I recommend this book to every young reader across the nation. Richardson is a fabulous author . . . and I certainly hope to read many more of her books. I thought *Indian Summer* was superb, and it kept me on the edge of my seat throughout the entire story.

—*Brenna Bales, Reader Views*

I loved this novel, which has a beautiful summer backdrop. It is fun, yet mysterious, and also delivers that all-important feeling of suspense. Certainly a book worth reading.

—*Jessica Roberts, Bookpleasures*

Tracy Richardson writes as if she remembers exactly how hard it is to fit in when you are Marcie's age. She also writes about life spent relaxing at a beach house. Marcie learns a lot that summer about growing up, and readers will learn along with her.

—*Shelley Wenger, TCM Reviews*

Is a new housing development inevitable progress, or are there important reasons to keep James Woods as it has been for millennia? Marcie's family values and the desire to be accepted by a wealthy, popular girl from school pull her in conflicting directions until she learns to choose for herself. Sailing details give a feeling of reality to this summer-at-the-lake story. At the same time, the sense of flying so strong it feels real and a bracelet that links the present with . . . Native American past lend a mystical flavor that carries readers beyond the ordinary.

—*LeAnne Hardy, author of* **Between Two Worlds** *and* **The Wooden Ox**

෮

SOMETHING IS CALLING her. Something in the water. She needs to find it. Raising her arms up from her sides she rises slowly into the air. She must go to James Bay. She flies over the water toward the dense and darkly green trees of the woods surrounding the bay. It is here with her now, trying to tell her something, but just beyond the edge of her consciousness. Her thoughts are reaching, trying to understand . . .

INDIAN SUMMER

❦ One ❦

MARCIE'S LEGS ACHE from pedaling up the Elm Street hill. She has to stand up the whole way using the weight of her body to push each pedal down, but now she's almost to the top. Only a few yards to go . . . and she's not getting off her bike to walk. It isn't really a hill anyway, but a bridge over the railroad tracks. The Indian Trail that winds through town runs beside the tracks at this point. Indians lived here long before any settlers came to this part of Indiana and the name of the town is an Indian word—Winnetka—which means beautiful land. Even the middle school that Marcie attends is called Indian Trail Middle School.

Today is the last day of school. *Maybe that's why I have the energy to ride my bike the whole way up the hill*, Marcie thinks. The last day of school means the annual Children's Fair! The entire town looks forward to the Children's Fair as the unofficial start of summer. She is so glad to be done with Mrs. Steadman's math class! The whole summer is before her. Except that there isn't much to look forward to. She's going to spend a few weeks at her Mamaw and Poppy's cottage on Lake Pappakeechee—it sounds like fun, and she used to love going to "the cottage," but this year everything feels different. None of her friends are coming, and it won't be as good with only her brothers. She's almost a teenager, and she still has to spend part of her summer with her grandparents and her brothers! Boring.

At the crest of the hill, Marcie pauses to catch her breath before starting the ride down. She can see the village green spread out below her at the bottom of the hill. Usually a wide open space surrounded by giant maple trees, it's now covered with tents and booths, banners and balloons, and is starting to fill up with people. School lets out after only a half day on the last day of the year, and everyone is converging on the green to enjoy the rest of the day at the Children's Fair.

Eric, her older brother, is near the bottom of the hill veering off in the direction of the bike racks. He's only two years ahead of her in school, but by the way he acts sometimes you'd think he was ten years older. Having an older brother is not as exciting as the kids at school seem to think. They are always telling her things like "I saw your brother at lunch," or "There's your brother, Marcie," as if she wants to keep tabs on him every moment of the day. She sees enough of him at home.

After the short rest, her breathing is almost back to normal and her legs don't feel so rubbery. She checks to make sure the coast is clear to begin her descent. It will spoil the ride if she has to stop to avoid hitting anyone. She starts by simply lifting her feet from the ground and onto the pedals, letting the weight of the bicycle start her moving down the hill.

The bike moves slowly at first, then rapidly picks up speed. The closer she gets to the bottom, the faster she goes. Marcie feels the wind whipping past her face and tugging at her clothes. She loves this feeling of freedom. *It feels like flying,* she thinks, and she realizes that her hands are no longer grasping the handle bars and her feet aren't touching the pedals. She can't feel the bike beneath her— she's soaring through the air—she is flying! She tentatively stretches out her arms and the wind lifts her up to the level of the treetops. Her bike is below, still speeding down the hill, and she is gliding high above it all. It feels so natural and effortless. She tries moving to the left and to the right by shifting her body and for a few moments she just enjoys the feeling of flying. Then she lowers her arms, which causes her to slowly descend back to her bike. Placing her hands on the handles and her feet on the pedals she continues the rest of the way down the hill on her bike. Just before the speed gets out of control—just before she gets afraid—Marcie puts on the brakes and comes to a stop. Turning to look back up the hill, she thinks, *did that really happen? Did I just fly?* It was only for a few moments, but she definitely felt herself flying. How could it possibly be real, though? She has dreamed of flying before, but nothing as real as this. It must have been some kind of daydream. The ride down the hill and the sensation of flying has left her a little breathless and shaky, so she walks her bike the rest of the way over to the bike racks.

She pulls up next to Eric as he locks his bike to the rack and slides her bike into the next space. She wants to ask him if he saw her flying, but doesn't know how to bring it up without sounding weird. Saying, 'By the way, Eric, did you see me flying down the hill just a minute ago' is just too strange. He wouldn't believe her if she told him what happened anyway. She's not really sure if she believes it herself.

Eric takes off his helmet and smoothes down his wavy brown hair. Marcie pulls her straight strawberry-blond hair back into a ponytail with the elastic on her wrist. The temperature was already nearing 85 degrees when they left the house after lunch and now she wants the hair off her neck.

"Hey, Marcie!" She turns to see her best friend, Sara, running toward them, and all thoughts of flying are forgotten. "Where have you been? The Fair started half an hour ago." Sara looks over at Eric and smiles.

Eric quickly glances at her while he scans the crowd for his friends.

"Mom made us empty our backpacks after school," Marcie says, "and put away all our stuff." Marcie straightens up after locking her bike to the rack. "When did you get here?"

"Twenty minutes ago." Sara says. "Hey, Eric, Jonathan and Will were here. They said to meet them at the hay bale maze." She pauses and pushes her hair behind her ear. "Or . . . you could come with us."

"Oh, uh, thanks, but . . . I think I'll catch up with them."

Just then someone yells, "Eric!" They turn to see Jonathan and Will in front of the snow cone stand.

"Great! I'll see you guys later." Eric calls over his shoulder as he practically runs over to meet his friends, his long legs covering the distance quickly.

Sara's glance lingers on Eric as he runs off, then she sighs and says, "Well, I tried. Anyway, the races don't start until three, so we have time to wander around first. Do you want to go to the Maze?"

"Sure," Marcie says. The walls constructed of hay bale "bricks" are to their right. As they walk over, Marcie says, in what she hopes is a casual tone, "Sara, you know Eric isn't much interested in having a girlfriend yet." Marcie wonders why anyone would want Eric as a boyfriend, but she doesn't say so to Sara.

"I know, but I can still hope!" Sara throws an imaginary tennis ball in the air and whacks it with an imaginary racquet. Marcie and Sara are on the track team at school, and Sara is also on the tennis team. They are running in the 100-meter dash for their age group this afternoon. "In two years we'll be in the high school age group for the races. Can you believe it?! Two more years until high school." Sara says "high school" with a mixture of trepidation and excitement.

"I know what you mean." She wonders how she will ever be ready for high school. She'd been worried about starting middle school and that had been fine, but high school seems different altogether.

Marcie has run in the races and won medals every year she can remember. They are displayed chronologically in a shadow box on the bookshelves in her room. The red, white, and blue ribbon of the first medal she won at age three is tattered and dirty from being worn constantly in the first few months. With each year the rows of ribbons are a little less shabby until three years ago when she stopped wearing them and just put the medals right into the box. The condition of the ribbons is as good as any picture to show her growing up. You couldn't see her getting older, but you knew it just the same.

Marcie gives herself a mental shake. She doesn't want to think about growing up today. "Let's go have some fun!"

THE GIRLS REACH the entrance to the hay bale maze. The walls of the maze are over their heads and it's easy to get disoriented. Sara starts into the maze first. Marcie follows a few minutes later. She rounds the twists and turns of the passageway and then stops when it branches off in two different directions.

Out of the corner of her eye she sees the figure of a dark-haired girl beckon to her to take the left hand path, but when she turns to look, the figure is gone. Thinking that it's Sara teasing her, Marcie starts running down the left-hand path and calls out, "Sara, wait up!" When she rounds the corner, the girl is disappearing around the next corner and Marcie can see that she has long hair in a pony-tail and is wearing a light-brown dress with beading on it. Puzzled, she realizes that it can't be Sara. Sara has shoulder length hair and is wearing shorts and a t-shirt. As she continues through the maze the girl is always just ahead of her at the next turn, and when there is a choice of which direction to take she is there to show her which way to go, but never letting Marcie get close enough to really see her or

9

talk to her. It's as if the girl is guiding Marcie through the maze, but always just out of reach. When Marcie rounds the last bend and can see the end of the maze, the girl isn't there. Thinking that she must have just come out of the maze, Marcie runs to catch her. She practically runs into Sara who is waiting for her at the exit doorway. The girl is gone.

"Hey! What's the big hurry?" asks Sara as she grabs onto Marcie's arms.

"How long have you been standing here? Did you see a girl just come out of the maze in a brown dress with her hair pulled back into a ponytail?"

"No, why?"

"I saw her in front of me in the maze. At first I thought it was you. She was always just ahead of me, and I could never catch up." Marcie pauses to catch her breath. "It was like she was guiding me through the maze. And her clothes were strange—she was barefoot and wearing a kind of tunic dress. It was really weird."

"It sounds weird, but I didn't see her. I don't know how she could have come out unless there are two ways to get to the end."

"That must be it. We must have come out by a different path than you did. That still doesn't explain why she was guiding me through the maze, though."

"Well, she's gone now. She was probably just messing with you. I'd forget about it."

"Yeah, I guess so." Marcie agrees, but she isn't really satisfied with that explanation.

When they hear the loudspeakers crackle and pop with the announcement for the beginning of the races, Sara is fastening a silvery metal necklace with a dolphin charm that Marcie won at one of the booths around Marcie's neck. She and Sara walk over to the monument where all the runners are gathered. They see her dad stretching against a tree. Marcie gets her speed from her dad, and he still likes to run in the annual races.

Casually, he says, "I thought I'd come by for the races since summer school doesn't start until next week. My schedule is flexible this afternoon." He's an English professor at the state university. Marcie isn't fooled. At breakfast this morning he had acted noncommittal about running in the races, but the rest of the family knew he couldn't stay away. "Good luck, ladies. See you at the finish line!"

Marcie and Sara go and stand under the banner for twelve year olds. Some of the other girls from the track team are there too. They all do a little stretching and warming up while the little kids have their races. The "track" is shortened for the preschoolers and the moms and dads stand at the finish line to cheer them on—and make sure they run in the right direction.

Finally their race is called. Marcie and Sara hold hands briefly and say "Good luck."

They line the girls up along the starting line. This race is just for fun, so there are no starting blocks, but Marcie still takes the racer's stance on one knee with her index finger and thumb aligned along the start line. She briefly looks over at the other girls. She knows most of them, but there are a few unfamiliar faces. Can she beat them? It seems like the whole town is watching the race from the sidelines. As usual before a race, her stomach flutters and her heart pounds in her chest.

The starter begins.

"On your mark," he shouts. Marcie holds herself still in the starting position.

"Get set." She comes up onto her hands and the balls of her feet.

"Go!" The starting gun explodes! Marcie pushes off with her feet and starts pumping with her arms as she rises up. In the beginning of a race all movement is slow motion. Like you are in one of those dreams where you are trying to run but can't because your legs are made of stone. Then suddenly she starts to go. Her fists are clenched. Arms reaching up and pulling back, up and back. Legs pounding—knees up, heels back, up and back, up and back. Kick, kick, kick. Faster, faster—she feels herself pulling away. Go, go, go, go!

She focuses on the finish line, feeling the fluid rhythm and power of her body. She imagines that she is pulling herself along a rope with her arms and kicking herself forward with her feet. Just a few more yards! She crosses the finish line first, a few steps ahead of the pack. Yes!

A volunteer with a gold banner across her chest runs toward Marcie, lifts her arm in the air and shouts, "First place!"

"Congratulations!" she says to Marcie. Sara's arm is held by a volunteer wearing a red banner that reads THIRD PLACE. Marcie gulps for air. The volunteers lead the winners over to the scorer's table and give them water bottles. Paula, another girl from the track team, has won second place. They give each other the team "high five." "Great job, Marce," says Sara between breaths, "but you always win."

Marcie feels a tug on her shirt. Looking down she sees her younger brother, Drew. "Great race, Marce, you were speedy," he says. Drew is seven and just finished first grade.

"Thanks, Drewster," says Marcie as she ruffles his sandy brown hair. "Mom!" she says as her mom comes up and gives her a hug.

"First place again!" her mom says smiling, the corners of her eyes crinkling into familiar laugh lines. Her strawberry blond hair, green eyes, and freckles were passed on to Marcie, but otherwise they don't really look alike. Marcie doesn't really look like either of her parents. More like a blending of both of their features. "Did you see your dad?" She winks at Marcie.

"Of course—he's by the monument waiting for his race." She indicates the direction with a nod of her head. They reach the scorer's table and Marcie turns to give her name to the woman seated in front of her. The woman exclaims to her mother, "Well hello, Jill. Is this first place winner your daughter?"

"Yes, this is Marcie." Turning to Marcie she says, "This is Abby Swyndall. Her husband is the new President of the university."

"Nice to meet you," replies Marcie. She feels a trickle of sweat run down her back between her shoulder blades and wishes she had something to wipe the sweat off her face.

Mrs. Swyndall asks, "Aren't you going into seventh grade in the fall?" Marcie nods. "My daughter Kaitlyn is in your grade. Do you know her?"

"Yes, she's in a couple of my classes." Marcie does know her, but after starting school last fall, Kaitlyn moved easily into the "popular" group, so they didn't socialize

14

much. She is momentarily distracted by Drew pulling on her shirt again to get her attention and tell her about the prizes he won that afternoon.

Over Drew's excited chatter, she hears her mom and Mrs. Swyndall talking. "Oh, yes, we'll be up at the lake this summer. Our summer house is finally finished, so we want to enjoy it," Mrs. Swyndall is saying. As she talks, her hands flutter in the air with a swirl of bright coral nail polish and the jangle of charms on her bracelet. "What about you?"

"Marcie and the boys are going to stay at my parents' cottage for a few weeks. I have a dig out west, and Paul will be working with his graduate students." Marcie's mom is an archaeologist and works part time at the university. Today she looks the part in khaki shorts, a light blue t-shirt, sandals, and a straw hat to shield the sun. Marcie thinks her mom looks casual and comfortable compared to Mrs. Swyndall in her flowered Capri pants and matching top. On the dig this summer Marcie's mom is taking a group of students to work on a new discovery of Native American sites in Utah. "We're going up there tomorrow to drop the kids off." Marcie's mom glances over at her. "This one isn't too excited because none of her friends can go this year."

"I have the perfect solution!" Mrs. Swyndall exclaims. "Kaitlyn is spending a few weeks at the lake with me and her older brother Kyle." She turns to Marcie. "This will work out so nicely—the two of you can get together." She taps her fingernails on the table. "We did a lot of sailing back east. We've joined the yacht club, but haven't met the other families yet. Do you sail?"

"Yes, we have a sunfish and a sloop," Marcie says. While thinking how unlikely it is that she and Kaitlyn will 'get together,' she sees Kaitlyn coming up behind Mrs. Swyndall. She is wearing super-short shorts and a top with spaghetti straps that would never have passed the school dress code. The school is always having to send home notes reminding everyone of the dress code, but it is really just the "popular" girls who push it to the limit.

"Mom," says Kaitlyn, acknowledging Marcie with a small wave of her hand, "I need more tickets."

"Sure, hon, there's money in my purse. We were just talking about you. You know Marcie Horton?" She barely pauses for Kaitlyn to reply as she rummages in the purse. "Marcie and her brothers will be spending a few weeks at the lake this summer while we're there. We thought you two could do some sailing together."

"Well . . . sure," says Kaitlyn cheerfully but a bit slowly. She looks at Marcie. "Have you ever sailed in the Regatta?"

The Regatta is a series of sailboat races over the Fourth of July weekend—a really big deal at the lake. The summer house crowd, or "Lakers," usually spend July Fourth at the lake and enter the races. They mostly belong to the Yacht Club, and over the years a rivalry between the Yacht Club crowd and the local residents has grown.

Marcie wonders if Kaitlyn thinks it was her idea to suggest getting together. "I've raced in the sunfish category, but our sloop isn't the right size for the big race. Eric started to crew for the Boat Company team last year." Marcie would love to be on the Boat Company Team, but it is just "the boys," as Eric likes to say. Eric and Marcie aren't technically Townies, because they don't live at the lake year round, but since their grandparents do and they aren't part of the yacht club crowd, they qualify. She wonders if the Swyndalls are aware of the rivalry.

"Really? We're going to enter our new E scow in the big race. Maybe you and Eric can crew with us." She pauses and seems to notice for the first time where she is. "Did you run in the races? You look all sweaty." She wrinkles her nose distastefully.

That's what happens when you exercise, thinks Marcie, but she says, "Yes, we just finished."

Mrs. Horton says, "She won first place!"

"Oh, right—aren't you on the track team? Uh, congratulations. The only time I get sweaty is when I lay out!" Kaitlyn says with a laugh. "Well, gotta go. The girls are waiting!"

17

"Always in a social whirl," Mrs. Swyndall says fondly to her daughter's retreating back. "Why don't you bring your family over for a cookout on Sunday afternoon, Jill? It'll be our first party at the cottage."

ও TWO ও

AFTER MARCIE CATCHES up with Sara, they decide to cool off under the shade of a nearby maple tree. As they are lounging in the grass in the dappled shade, Marcie wonders about Kaitlyn and her family. Kaitlyn is nice enough most of the time, unlike some of the other "popular" girls, but she can be stuck-up, too. Marcie has always wanted to compete in the big race, but for a Laker team and with Kaitlyn Swyndall? Still . . . to be in the race, it could be worth it. Maybe Kaitlyn is okay when she's on her own, and Marcie's parents do know Kaitlyn's parents from the university where Mr. Swyndall took over as president a little over a year ago. The families don't socialize much outside of university functions—although that could change now that the Swyndalls have a house on the lake. They bought the old James place on Lake Pappakeechee after Mrs. James passed away. The property includes acres of woods and marsh where all the kids play explorers and capture the flag. The Swyndalls immediately tore down the little bungalow on the property and built a giant—and beautiful—new vacation house. When her family drove by it the last time she was at the lake, Marcie's Mamaw smiled ruefully and called it a "McMansion." It does look a little strange and out of place next to the older, smaller cottage on the property next door.

Her thoughts are interrupted when Annie Crawford plops down on the grass with her and Sara.

"What're you doing laying around here?" says Annie. "Eat too much cotton candy?" She laughs a little too loud and smacks Marcie on the leg hard enough that it stings.

"Annie, that hurt!" says Marcie, "and no, we didn't eat too much cotton candy. We just ran in the races."

"Marcie won first place—again," says Sara pretending to pout.

"Well la-dee-da," says Annie. She grabs Sara's arm and tries to pull her up. "Come with me to the Moon Walk!" she wheedles.

Annie's trouble, thinks Marcie, is that she tries so hard to make friends that she is annoying. Sara and Marcie aren't really good friends with her, but they might be the only friends Annie has at school, so they try to be nice to her. A shadow falls over them and they look up to see Ashley, Meghan, and Bailey, three of Marcie's least favorite popular girls, standing in front of them. Ashley, with straight brown hair and wide-set brown eyes, is the ringleader. She says, "Annie, when are you going to get those bracelets you promised us?" She has her hands on her hips and her eyebrows raised mockingly. The other two girls say "Yeah," in unison. Marcie thinks they look like clones of each other, or the three mean musketeers.

"Well, I, uh, don't have them," Annie stammers.

"That's what I thought," says Ashley. She looks knowingly at the others. "You never did have them. You're just a little liar."

It's obvious that Ashley is about to say more, but Sara stands up, glares directly at Ashley and says, "Why don't you leave her alone, Ashley Barnes. Go and buy your own bracelets."

Ashley catches her breath and takes a step back. She isn't used to being confronted. "Yeah, well, maybe I will, since we're obviously not getting any from her." She recovers herself and glances in Marcie's direction. "Nice necklace," she says, sarcastically referring to the silvery dolphin necklace encircling her neck. "I saw they were giving those away at the baby games." Marcie covers the necklace with her hand and opens her mouth to say something in reply, but no sound comes out. At that moment, Kaitlyn approaches the group, saying, "Well, I think it's a nice necklace. I've always liked dolphins."

"Huh!" says Ashley. To Meghan and Bailey she says, "Let's get out of here. This is totally boring." They turn and saunter off.

"Just ignore her," Kaitlyn says to Marcie. "See you at the lake!" and she walks off after the other three girls.

"Thanks, Sara," says Annie, letting out a big sigh. "I told them I would bring back bracelets from our spring break trip to Florida, but my mom wouldn't let me." Her lower lip quivers a little. "She said I was buying friends. They've been bugging me ever since."

"Who needs friends like that?" Sara scoffs as she sits back down on the grass.

"That was so great Sara!" says Marcie, a bit too enthusiastically. "You really told her off!" She hopes they don't realize how flustered Ashley made her feel.

"What's up with Kaitlyn?" asks Sara. "I didn't know you two were friends."

"We aren't, really. Her family will be at the lake when I'm there this summer, and our moms suggested we go sailing together. Not that we will or anything!" Marcie wonders again about the race and what it would be like go to the Pappakeechee Yacht Club. She also wonders why Kaitlyn stood up for her.

"How can you be so brave?" Annie asks Sara.

"It's no big deal. She deserved it. I was just making good Karma."

"Good Karma? What's that?"

"It kind of means, 'what goes around comes around.' Like if you do a good thing, good things will happen to you and if you do a bad or mean thing, bad things will happen to you. My mom told me about it." Sara's mom is Indian—from India. That's where Sara gets her smooth dark hair and eyes like pools of ink.

"Well, those three should have a lot of bad things happen to them!" laughs Marcie.

Marcie, Sara, and Annie decide to go to the Moon Walk before Marcie has to go home for dinner.

On the way over, Marcie wishes she could be as brave as Sara. Why can't she stand up to Ashley like that? She is afraid of becoming a target herself, that's why. Sara seems to be immune to it. Perhaps having exotic good looks helps her to be so confident, thinks Marcie. Her own snub nose and freckles certainly don't give her a feeling of confidence. It doesn't hurt that Sara's dad's side of the family is one of the oldest and most respected families in Winnetka. Not to mention the wealthiest. You'd never know it, though, from how they act. They're not stuck-up at all. In fact, Mr. Clements is an attorney for one of those environmental watch-dog groups. But Marcie thinks it's more than that. Sara would be comfortable with who she is no matter what. *Why aren't I comfortable with myself like that?* Marcie wonders.

❧ Three ❧

THE SCREEN DOOR bangs closed behind Marcie as she comes in through the back door to the kitchen. It startles their Cairn terrier, Speck, who is sleeping in his favorite armchair in the family room. He comes tearing over to Marcie yapping wildly. His nails can't get purchase on the wood floor so he skitters past her in his rush. She stoops to pick him up. "It's only me, Speck." He stops barking and begins licking her face with his little pink tongue.

"Oh, good. You're just in time." Her mom is washing her hands at the sink. "Are you on table-setting or clean-up this month?"

"Setting. What're we having?" Marcie puts Speck down in his chair, and he rests his head on the arm to watch them. She washes her hands in the sink and then gathers up silverware and napkins and starts to set the table in the dining room where they usually have dinner. Her mom says it makes the evening meal more special than always eating in the kitchen.

"I thought we'd have spaghetti and meatballs since it's our last family meal together at home for a while." A little louder she says, "Dinner's ready!"

Her dad calls out, "Coming!" from his office off the family room. Eric's footsteps can be heard pounding down the stairs. The Hortons' house is in town, where many of the faculty live. The neighborhood was built in the 1920s, so the houses are older and a bit creaky, but they have high ceilings, crown molding, and wood floors; as Mom says, they have character. No two houses are alike. Back when the house was originally built, they didn't have family rooms or big kitchens, so somewhere along the line an addition was built on to the back, enlarging the kitchen and adding a family room and an office. The neighborhood also has mature trees. Not like out in the subdivisions built on what used to be cornfields where none of the trees are over 15 feet tall. Marcie can't imagine not having the trees. They make her feel safe somehow. Like giant sentinels sheltering and watching over them. She always thinks it is sad when she rides her bike past one of the original farm houses in the area and reads the sign posted on the picket fence that says INDIANA FAMILY FARM HOMESTEAD. OWNED BY THE SAME FAMILY FOR OVER 100 YEARS. Now it is in the middle of a sprawling subdivision surrounded by cookie-cutter houses.

At dinner they talk about going to the lake in the morning. Marcie says, "I don't know why we can't just stay here. Dad will be here, and we're old enough to be on our own."

"Drew is not old enough to be left unsupervised, and I don't want you and Eric to be at loose ends," Mrs. Horton says, dabbing her mouth with her napkin. "Your dad will be busy with his graduate students and won't be able to keep an eye on Drew. We've been through all this before. We're lucky to have a place like Lake Pappakeechee to go to and grandparents who want you to stay with them."

"I want to go," says Drew. "Poppy is going to take me fishing."

"So do I," says Eric. "Why are you whining about going? It'll be great!"

"Great for you, maybe. You can do stuff with your friends at the Boat Company, but the only person I know will be Kaitlyn Swyndall!" says Marcie shrilly. "And I am not whining, you dork!"

"That's enough, Marcie. You too, Eric," says their dad. "I'm sorry that none of your friends can go this year, Marce, but this is the best solution for our family. You've always enjoyed going before."

"It's just not fair!" She slams the palms of her hands down on the table, making the dishes clatter and water slosh over the glasses. She isn't sure why she is feeling so upset. Perhaps it's the encounter with the girls at the fair, or maybe she's worrying about seeing Kaitlyn at the lake. It feels like her insides are boiling and they are going to rise up and choke her. "If Mom weren't going to Utah, we wouldn't have to go. Why do you have to work anyway? Why can't you stay home like some of the other moms?" She knows she is going overboard, but she can't seem to stop herself. "It's all your fault!"

There is a stunned silence at the table. Her mom looks at Marcie thoughtfully. Her Dad finally says, "Why don't you go upstairs until you can cool down. You can finish your dinner later."

"I'm finished now!" she says, flinging her napkin down on the table and rushing upstairs to her room.

She throws herself down on her bed and buries her head in the pillows. Why did she act that way? She hadn't intended to, but something just came over her and now she has spoiled their family dinner. What's the matter with her? Going to stay at her grandparents' cottage had always been something to look forward to. Lately she can't seem to sort anything out. She feels something cold and wet in her ear. Reaching up, she touches Speck's silky hair, and turns her head toward him. *You love me, don't you?* she thinks. He starts licking away her salty tears. After a few minutes she starts to feel better. There is a knock on her door and her mom says, "Can I come in?"

"Okay," says Marcie quietly. Her mother comes in and sits on the edge of the bed. She reaches over and smoothes Marcie's hair. "Do you want to talk?" she asks.

Marcie sits up and turns toward her mom. "I'm sorry, Mom. I don't know what's wrong with me! Sometimes I feel like I'm on a roller coaster ride. Part of me really wants to go to the lake and part of me doesn't."

"I'm sorry too, honey. I wish I could go with you to the lake, but I also like my job. It's part of who I am." She wipes away the remaining tears on Marcie's face. "Being confused is part of growing up and dealing with new emotions and changing responsibilities. You'll work it out. It just takes time."

"Speck came up to comfort me. He always seems to know when I'm upset."

"Yes," says her mom, scratching the little dog's head. "Speck does have a kind of intuition, doesn't he?" Speck rolls over onto his back to get his belly rubbed. "Makes me think of that tsunami wave that hit India and Sumatra a while back. Remember no animals were found dead? It's like the animals could sense the wave coming and got out of the way. Isn't it strange—and sad, really—that with all of our technology, we humans were caught by surprise."

"Didn't the elephants run into the hills with tourists on their backs?" Marcie asks.

"That's right—I think there was even a story about a dog helping to rescue a boy by chasing him out of a hut where he was hiding and herding him up to the hills."

"I know Speck would rescue me." Marcie picks him up and cuddles him. "Do you think people can 'sense' things like animals can?"

"Yes, I do. After studying the Native Americans all these years, it's become pretty clear to me that they may not have had all the technology and material stuff we do, but they were much more connected to the natural world. I've also read and heard some amazing stories about aboriginal tribes living now in Australia and South America who have abilities that we can't explain with modern science."

"Like what?"

"They have an inter-connectedness between the members of the tribe and to the world around them. They can communicate without words. Also, they seem to have a knowledge and understanding of what will happen in the future, or what did happen in the distant past," says her mom.

"It sounds like they're psychic or something."

"It's like psychic powers. We used to call it ESP, Extra-Sensory Perception—perceiving or understanding things outside of your five senses." She shifts her position on

Marcie's bed. "The difference is that instead of being limited to certain people, the entire tribe has these abilities."

"So, maybe everyone has a 'sixth sense,' but we don't know how to use it," Marcie says reflectively.

"That's what I think. We just need to give ourselves some time and space to be quiet. Sometimes quiet is hard to come by," says her mom. "Well," she sighs, sits up and places her hands on her thighs, "I need to finish packing for my trip out west. Are you all set?"

"Pretty much. I just have to do shampoo and bathroom stuff." She pauses and lets out her breath. "Thanks, Mom. I love you."

"I love you, sweetheart. I'm going to miss you." She gives Marcie a hug.

"I'll miss you too. Will you call us?"

"I'll try to call every few days, and I'll be thinking about you. Moms have a kind of intuition, too, you know."

MARCIE STRETCHES OUT on her bed with her arms behind her head. Her eyes fall on the her race medals and ribbons. She loves the exhilarating feeling of running. The wind rushing past her, the feeling of speed. It feels almost like—

flying. Could she really have been flying that afternoon? It sure felt real when it was happening.

After a while, when she feels calmer, Marcie goes in the bathroom to wash her face. As she splashes water to rinse off the soap and reaches for a towel, she catches her reflection in the mirror. It's not a bad face, she thinks, just ordinary. But she doesn't want to be ordinary, and she doesn't feel ordinary inside. She feels different; even special. Maybe everyone feels that way. She sucks in her cheeks creating hollows beneath the bones and turns her head to the side. That's better, more dramatic. Then she lets out her breath and her face returns to normal. Back to ordinary, everyday Marcie.

As she turns away from the mirror, she catches a glimpse of a second reflection out of the corner of her eye. It is so fleeting that she's not even sure it was really there. She had the briefest glimpse of the face of a girl with a darker complexion, deep brown eyes, and black hair pulled behind her head. When Marcie turns back to face the mirror, there is only her own reflection, green eyes gazing back at her. She reaches out to touch the mirror with her fingertips, as if it might not be entirely solid, and encounters the reassuring, smooth surface of the glass. *What's going on?* she wonders.

CRICKETS ARE BUZZING and lightning bugs flash on and off over the lawn as Marcie crosses the back yard looking for her dad. It is not as hot as during the day, but humidity still hangs heavy in the air and the cool grass feels wonderful on her bare feet. The night is clear. Looking up, she sees the sky is filled with stars. Sometimes her dad will load the family into the van and drive everyone out to the country to star gaze with his telescope. Marcie finds it hard to imagine that all those pinpoints of light are stars like our own sun and that each of them is part of its own solar system. The Universe is so huge. Just thinking about it puts her little problems in her little world into perspective. But surprisingly, instead of feeling diminished, she finds it comforting. She is part of the Universe—granted, a tiny, confused part, but still somehow connected. Maybe she's even a vital part—who's to say?

She finds her dad in front of the garage with Drew, raising the seat on Drew's bicycle. The light of the overhead floodlights makes crazy shadows on the driveway. Five shadows of Dad going from dark to light all move in unison as he loosens the bolts on the bike. "Hi, Dad." She stops in front of him. "I'm sorry about dinner."

"Oh, honey, that's okay." He puts down his tools and stands up to give her a hug. "You were just having a bad moment. If you can't get upset with your family, who can you get upset with? I'm glad you're feeling better." He starts to tickle her.

"Hey, Dad—stop it! I'm not a baby anymore, you know," she says, half laughing, half annoyed.

"You will always be my baby." He puts his hands on her shoulders. "It's hard to remember that you're already twelve years old. Almost a teenager. It seems like just yesterday you had training wheels on your bike."

"Look, Marcie," says Drew, "Dad is making my bike bigger because I'm getting bigger!"

"You sure are," says Marcie. Her dad gets back to work on the bike and they sit in comfortable silence for a few minutes. Then Drew says suddenly, "Dad, are we poor?"

Their dad looks up at Drew with a puzzled and amused expression on his face. "Poor? No, we're not poor."

"Are we rich?"

"No, we're not rich, either. We're just right. Why do you ask?"

"Joey says we must be poor since you drive a junky old car instead of a new car like his dad."

"I see." He pauses. "Well, I drive this junky old car," he says with a grin, gesturing toward his car parked behind them in the garage, "because I choose to drive it, not because we can't afford to buy a new one. It runs just fine and it's not important to me to have a new car. Part of the reason that we do have money in the bank is because we don't spend money on things we don't really need. Does that make sense?"

"I guess so. Kind of like when I spend my allowance on candy and then I don't have any money to buy the game I've been wanting?"

"Yes, that's it exactly." He and Marcie exchange a look over Drew's head. It's a family joke that Drew has a hard time saving any of his allowance. As soon as he gets any money accumulated, he's asking one of them to take him to the store so he can buy something. She has to admit though, that it is a bit embarrassing to ride in Dad's car. Especially if he's giving one of her friends a ride.

"Alright, buddy. It's time for you to get in bed. We're leaving after lunch tomorrow for Mamaw and Poppy's."

"Yippee!" says Drew and he starts skipping toward the house. Marcie and her dad follow more slowly behind him and Marcie slips her hand through her dad's arm.

❧ Four ❧

THE DRIVE TO the cottage only takes about two hours. Just the perfect amount of time to read or take a nap, but not get totally bored. They leave right after lunch and get there with plenty of the day still to enjoy. As soon as the van stops they all pile out and stretch and there is Mamaw at the back door to greet them, her tall, angular frame filling the doorway. The sweet, vanilla smell of baking wafts past her from the kitchen.

"Hello, Lilly," says Dad giving her a kiss on the cheek. "What is that wonderful smell?"

"Mamaw!" calls Drew, running over to her.

"I bought some strawberries at the farmers' market this morning, so I thought I'd make shortcake for dessert. Poppy is going to do a fish fry for dinner. He's down at the pier now catching a few more fish—we hope! He could probably use some help," she says to the kids.

A fish fry and Mamaw's strawberry shortcake from scratch—she always makes real whipped cream—Marcie's mouth starts to water. "Hello Drew!" Mamaw bends over to give Drew a hug. Her short salt and pepper hair contrasts with his sandy blond hair. "We're so glad you're all here. You kids know where you're sleeping. I cleaned out drawers for your stuff, but you can unpack later." She hugs the rest of them and adds, "Aunt Lucy and Uncle Mark will be over later this afternoon when the little ones get up from their naps. Come see the garden, Jill." She and Marcie's mom start to walk away.

"I'd love that, Mom," says Mrs. Horton.

"Hang on! Before you all rush off and leave me," Dad holds up his hands, "everyone grab your bags and bring them to your room, and then you can go do your thing."

Eric grabs his stuff and bounds into the house with Drew close behind. Marcie follows more slowly. It feels good to be at the cottage. Like having a beautiful and familiar quilt wrap around you. Why didn't she want to come? It all seems so unimportant now. Going in through the back door to the mud room, Marcie turns to her right and up the stairs to the kids' sleeping loft. The house doesn't really have a front and back door. What you would think of as the back of the house with the kitchen actually faces the street and the part of the house facing the lake is a big sunroom with windows all around to take advantage of the water views. At the top of the stairs, she pauses. Directly in front of her is the big arched window facing the lake with its window seat covered in faded cushions.

The window seat is Marcie's favorite place to read or be alone. She catches a glimpse of the water beyond and happiness floods through her. She's at the cottage! George, the big black-and-white calico cat, is lying on the seat in the sun. He is easily twice as big as Speck and very lazy. He's also fifteen years old. The boys drop off their suitcases by their usual beds and swing round the newel post at the top of the stairs on their way back downstairs. "We're going fishing with Poppy. Want to come?" says Eric. He's been nicer to her today after calling her a whiner at dinner last night.

"Not right now," she replies. She wants to unpack her things and settle in a bit before going downstairs.

"Okay—later!"

Once they're gone, Marcie opens the drawers under her bunk and puts her things away. She always sleeps on the bottom bed of the single bunk along one side of the room. It's "her" bed. The boys like the top beds of the other two bunks across the room, but Marcie thinks the bottom is more cozy. It feels like a cave. Her quilt is a multi-colored plaid this time, faded from frequent washing, and smelling of fresh air and sunshine from drying on the clothesline. She puts her books on the shelves beside her bed, stows her suitcase in the closet, and sits next to George on the window seat. A deep, rumbling emanates from his chest and he stretches luxuriously.

The windows are open and the fan suspended from the vaulted ceiling is turned on so there is a nice breeze. She can smell the water—clean, fresh, alive. Marcie always thinks of the color green when she smells the lake. It's how she imagines green would smell. The sun glinting on the surface of the water seems to be calling to her. She decides to go for a swim. She changes into her suit and grabs a towel from under the sink. Can't forget the sunscreen—she grabs that, too. Her mom's an absolute fanatic about using sunscreen—fair skin and freckles do tend to burn.

On her way to the pier, she passes her dad already napping in the hammock slung between two oak trees in the garden and hears a familiar bark behind her. She smiles to herself and turns to see their elderly neighbor, Al, and his dog Pansy ambling toward her. "Hi, Al!" she says. Pansy is so happy to see Marcie that her whole body is wagging, but she sits and waits for Marcie to come over and pet her. "Hello, good girl, how are you?" Marcie ruffles her ears and is rewarded with a big, wet kiss. Pansy's fur is brown tipped with black and the light brown markings on her face are in the shape of a pansy, like two big petals around her eyes. Her mouth curls up in the back so she always looks like she's grinning at you.

"I heard the commotion and thought I would find you Hortons down here," says Al. "Actually, it was Pansy who couldn't wait. I was having a nap, but she insisted I get up and bring her out to say Hello." He pats her head fondly. Al is the unofficial mayor of the neighborhood, and Marcie could have predicted that he'd be over right away to welcome them to the lake. He knows everything going on around the cove and checks in with everyone regularly. He's been a friend of the family for as long as she can remember. When she and Eric were little they would toddle over to his house to sit with him on his porch swing or to play darts or checkers. Actually, they still go over to visit with him. The fact that he has a tin full of candy at the ready for visiting children isn't the only reason they want to go. He is always happy to see them and spend time visiting.

The boys see Al and wave. "Catch anything?" he calls to them.

"Drew caught two, but I haven't had a bite!" replies Eric. Marcie and Al have almost reached the pier.

"Would you three like to go to James Bay with me to fish tomorrow?" asks Al.

"Yes! You bet! Oh, Yeah!" they shout at the same time.

"Maybe we can go in the morning and pack a picnic lunch. How does that sound?"

"Great!" they all answer. James Bay is their special place. It's quiet by the shore and the marshy waters are filled with birds, turtles, and otters. It's a great fishing spot.

"Have a seat, Al." says Poppy indicating a lawn chair.

"Don't mind if I do." Al ambles to the chair, easing himself onto the seat, and Pansy sits beside him. Turning to Marcie, Poppy says, "Hey, you! I wondered when you'd be down." He sees her towel and bathing suit. "Going swimming? The water's perfect—nice and warm." He nods toward the green-blue water with his ever present baseball cap, which covers his almost completely bald scalp.

Marcie gets a big inner tube from the shed and slides into it from the dock. Floating out in the channel she feels the water relaxing her body. It is so great not having to be anywhere or do anything in particular, she thinks. No homework, no after school activities, nothing. Eventually, Drew and Eric join her and they spend the afternoon zipping down the slide, doing silly jumps off the diving board, and floating on the water. When Aunt Lucy and Uncle Mark arrive with three-year-old Michael and baby Janey, Michael wants to swim with the big kids. He idolizes Eric and Drew, the "big boys," and wants to play with them every chance he gets.

"Be sure to keep an eye on him, will you?" Lucy says. "I'll put his life jacket on him, but you still have to be careful."

"No problem," calls Eric, floating on his back on an inflatable raft. "Send him down the slide and I'll catch him!"

"I can do it myself, Mom." Michael shimmies up the stairs and lets out a squeal of delight on his way down the slide before he lands with a splash in the lake.

❧ Five ❧

AFTER THE DINNER dishes are cleaned up and the guys have settled in to watch a ball game, Mamaw suggests taking an evening stroll. On the walk back home, as they turn the corner onto their street, Marcie looks up to see a shiny, dark blue convertible pulling into the driveway of the cottage. *Who could that be?* she wonders. The driver is a man, a woman is in the passenger seat, and a girl sits in the back seat. Getting closer, she sees that it's Kaitlyn Swyndall in the back, and it looks like Mrs. Swyndall in the front seat, so Mr. Swyndall must be behind the steering wheel.

Her dad has come out of the house and is shaking hands with Mr. Swyndall as the four of them return from the walk and come up the drive. "Hallo there, Hortons!" booms out Mr. Swyndall. "Out for an evening walk? We thought we'd take a little drive ourselves. I wanted to take my new toy out for a spin." He pats the hood of the car.

"It's a beauty," says her dad, with an admiring tone, although Marcie knows he isn't much interested in cars.

After glancing at Mamaw as though in silent confirmation, Marcie's mom says, "Hello, Abby, Don and you too,

Kaitlyn. You have perfect timing! We were just going to enjoy some strawberry shortcake. It's my mom's home-made recipe. Why don't you come in and join us?"

"Are you sure it's no trouble?" asks Abby Swyndall.

"Not at all," says Mamaw. "I always make extra. Come on in."

The adults get out of the car through the doors and Kaitlyn hops nimbly over the side onto the drive.

"Hey," says Marcie to Kaitlyn. She hadn't expected to see her so soon after arriving at the cottage. She feels a little unsure about how to act around her.

"Hi," replies Kaitlyn. They stand uncertainly, facing each other. Marcie realizes that Kaitlyn feels uncomfortable, too, but she's not sure what to do. Seeing their discomfort, her mom says, "Marcie, why don't you and Kaitlyn help serve the shortcake?" She holds open the screen door for them and adds. "You can make the whipped cream."

"Okay," says Marcie, relieved. She shoots her mom a grateful look as the girls pass her going into the kitchen. "Here Kaitlyn," opening a cabinet door she gestures to the dishes inside. "Plates are in there and silverware is in the drawer below. I'll get the strawberries and whipping cream. The shortcakes are on the counter." She pulls open the refrigerator and scoops up the bowl of sliced strawberries and carton of whipping cream. The adults have ga-

thered in the sunroom on the chairs and couches surrounding the low wooden farm table. She can hear Mamaw asking if anyone would like coffee.

"You can cook? I don't know how to make whipped
cream. Or anything else for that matter," says Kaitlyn with
a laugh. "How many plates?"

"There are eleven of us, not including the baby, so the
three of you will make fourteen." Marcie plugs in the port-
able mixer and pours the cream into a mixing bowl. "I
help my mom and Mamaw in the kitchen sometimes, but I
don't do a lot of cooking on my own. Whipped cream is
easy. It's just whipping cream and sugar."

"My mom doesn't really cook much. We mostly just
fend for ourselves. Prepackaged stuff. I'm great with the
microwave!" says Kaitlyn as she counts plates and silverware. Marcie measures the sugar and pours it into the
bowl with the cream. The whir of the electric mixer momentarily discourages more conversation.

When everyone is served, the girls go sit on the deck
outside the sunroom to enjoy their dessert. Eric, Drew,
and little Michael are already there. "This is really good!"
exclaims Kaitlyn.

"Yeah, homemade is the best," says Marcie through a
mouthful of strawberries, cream, and shortcake. Inside,
the adults are having a similar conversation. Mrs. Swyndall
says, "This is really delicious, but I can really only have a

bite. Always watching my weight!" she pats her waist. "I don't do much cooking, what with all of my volunteering and fundraising activities. Luckily, the new gourmet market in town has a good bakery." Kaitlyn rolls her eyes at Marcie and says, "What'd I tell you?" under her breath.

"Your house is so darling, Lilly. Did you use a decorator?" Mrs. Swyndall continues.

"No, we did it ourselves little by little over the years," says Mamaw.

"Well, you did a terrific job. I had our cottage professionally decorated since we needed it finished quickly. We do so much entertaining with Don's position at the university."

Don Swyndall joins the conversation, asking Poppy, "How much land do you have here?"

"About five acres, including the woods and gardens," says Poppy.

"Have you ever considered selling some of the woods to a developer?" Mr. Swyndall leans forward towards Poppy and gestures at him with his fork. "You're sitting on a gold mine. It could really increase your property value." Marcie's ears perk up—sell the woods!?

"Oh, we would never sell." Poppy waves his hand in an arc indicating the house and yard. "We value our property just the way it is," he says with a chuckle. Marcie relaxes. She likes the lake cottage just the way it is, too.

Al clears his throat and sits up straighter. Pansy lifts her head beside his chair. "Didn't I hear that you are planning to do some more development on the property you just bought—in James Woods?" he asks Don Swyndall in a deceptively light and friendly tone. "You've got what—ten to fifteen acres?"

"Oh, we've looked into different options, but nothing definite. I think a walking and biking path would be a nice idea, and perhaps some public areas," says Mr. Swyndall vaguely.

"Oh, I'm glad to hear that," says Mamaw. "So much of the woods around the lake have already been developed. There are only a few areas of wetlands and woods left as natural habitat for the birds and wildlife." Al doesn't say any more, but his brow is furrowed and he looks thoughtful.

"Well, more and more people are looking at their lake property as an investment." Mr. Swyndall leans back in his chair and crosses his legs. "We got a steal on our place," he says smugly. "Tearing down that old house and building our 'cottage' increased our property value considerably."

Kaitlyn leans over to Marcie and says, "All my dad ever talks about is money. It's totally annoying. Let's go see your room."

Marcie is a little stunned by the conversation she overheard. She had no idea there was talk of changing James Woods. It's their special place! "Oh, okay," she says distractedly. "This way, through the kitchen. We'll leave our plates in the sink." She leads Kaitlyn up the stairway to the loft.

When they get to the top of the stairs, Kaitlyn says, "This is so cute—a loft! But where's your room?"

"This is my room," replies Marcie. "It's the kids' sleeping loft. The cottage isn't big enough for us to have separate bedrooms," she says.

"But you don't have any privacy! I would hate to share a room with Kyle. I don't want him to mess with my stuff." She sits down on the window seat and leans back on the cushions. "Where do you keep all your things?"

"I have drawers under my bed and shelves next to it," says Marcie. "I don't really need a lot of things at the lake." She feels annoyed at Kaitlyn for criticizing the loft and embarrassed about it at the same time. "I love sleeping up here. It feels like being at camp," she says a little defensively. She pulls a wicker rocking chair next to the window seat and puts her feet on the edge of the cushion so she can rock herself.

"Oh, it's really quaint, you know, old-fashioned. I guess I was just expecting that you'd have your own room, like I do. You can see it tomorrow when your family comes over for the cookout." She looks out the window. The boys are in the yard below playing whiffle ball. Kaitlyn cocks her head to one side and looks at Marcie. "I talked to Kyle about the July 4th Regatta. Do you still want to be on a team with us? He has a friend who wants to, and with you we'll have a crew of four."

In her mind, Marcie is still unsure about sailing on a Laker team, but she surprises herself by saying, "Yes, I do want to be on the team. It'll be fun." There. She'd done it.

"Great," says Kaitlyn, clapping her hands together. "You can come over during the week to practice. I don't think we're ready to race in tomorrow's Sunday Regatta, but we'll be ready for the big race on the Fourth. We could even win!" Her face breaks into a big smile. "That would be sooo cool!"

"Yeah," says Marcie smiling back. "That would be cool." The competitive side of her, the part that drives her to win when she runs, warms to the idea. *It would be totally cool to win*, she thinks.

"What about Monday or Tuesday?" asks Kaitlyn. "Can you come over then?"

"I'll have to let you know tomorrow. I'm not sure what's going on yet."

Her mom calls up the stairs just then, "Girls, the Swyndalls are getting ready to leave now. Come on down."

"Okay, mom." Standing up she says to Kaitlyn, "Well, I guess I'll see you tomorrow."

They walk downstairs, and everyone says their good-byes. As she watches the Swyndalls drive away, Marcie's thoughts are only on the sailboat race. She has completely forgotten about what Mr. Swyndall might do to James Woods. At least, for the moment.

↷ Six ↷

THAT NIGHT, MARCIE dreams of flying. Earlier in the evening, after the Swyndalls left, she helped get Michael ready for bed while Lucy was busy with Janey. She got him a drink of milk in the kitchen and then herded him through the living room to the bedrooms on the other side of the house. Her grandparents use the largest of the three bedrooms, and her parents and Aunt and Uncle each take the other two. Janey is still in a crib, so she sleeps in the room with Mark and Lucy, but Michael is one of the "big kids" and sleeps in the loft. As she was putting on his pajamas, Michael said, "Can you fly, Marcie?"

She had been taken aback by his question and answered without thinking. "No, I can't fly, silly." But she remembered when she had the sensation of flying while riding her bike to the Children's Fair and the vivid flying dreams she sometimes has had. "Why do you ask?"

"I can fly," said Michael matter-of-factly. "I fly around my back yard. I lift up my arms and go up into the air. I can fly over the trees. Sometimes I forget how, though, right Mommy?" Lucy walked into the bedroom carrying

Janey, fresh from her bath, wrapped in a hooded duck towel.

"Are you telling Marcie about flying, sweetheart?" She reached into the cabinet to get a diaper. "Michael says the most amazing things. It's unusual enough that he talks so well, but the things he says!" she whispered to Marcie. "Last week I found him out in the yard running fast and trying to fly. He was pretty upset. When I asked him what he was playing, he said 'Mommy, why can't I fly anymore? I know I could fly around the yard before.' I didn't really know what to say. I told him that maybe it was a dream or maybe he imagined it, but he was certain that he had flown before." A prickly sensation went up Marcie's spine. How weird. It was just like her flying dreams. They seem so real that when she wakes up she wonders if maybe she really can fly. As she got older she didn't think they were real anymore, but the feeling was hard to shake all the same. She thinks about it for a long time before falling asleep. Maybe that's what triggers the dream.

In her dream, Marcie is standing outside the cottage under the maple tree. It's nighttime; the stars are flickering through the leaves overhead. She still has on the pajama top and shorts she wore to bed. She doesn't know how she got here, maybe she was sleeping and came outside, but it doesn't seem to matter. Something is calling her. Something in the water. She needs to find it. Raising her arms up from her sides she rises slowly into the air. She doesn't have to flap her arms, she simply thinks that she wants to fly and her body rises into the air. Dream flying is just how you imagine it will be—head up, arms out to the side, legs and torso straight out behind. Effortless.

She hovers under the protecting limbs of the tree for a moment and then glides over the lawn and the boat docks to the lake. The moon shines down on the water beneath her as if illuminating her path and the gentle ripples of the water encourage her onward. Something is telling her to go to James Bay, and her thoughts cause her to turn in that direction. The dream isn't frightening. On the contrary, she feels happy and relaxed, but there's an insistent need to go out over the lake. It is quiet and deserted at first, but then, as sometimes happens in dreams, it changes from night into the middle of the day, and Marcie is flying over sailboats and water sparking with sunlight. She is close enough to the boats that she can hear the wind luffing in the sails and people calling to each other. The boats are rounding a big orange buoy floating in the water. Colorful spinnaker sails that always remind her of parachutes unfurl to catch the wind as the boats change direction and go downwind. Whoosh! A bright orange sail balloons out on the front of the boat directly below her, and Marcie rises higher into the sky. This must be the Sunday Regatta, she is aware of thinking, but she can't stop to watch. She must go to James Bay. She flies on.

She rounds Owen Point and enters the bay. The dense and darkly green trees of James Woods are before her across the bay leading down to the cattails and reeds of the marshy shore. She stops and hovers over the water in the center of the bay. There is something she needs to find, but what? The water glimmers beneath her, and the tops of the trees sway in the breeze. She feels like whatever is calling her is here with her, and the image is just at the edge of her mind, eluding her. If only she could concentrate more on the picture, reach out her thoughts to grasp it . . .

Suddenly, the dream ends and she wakes up in her bed in the loft. At first she is disoriented and doesn't know where she is. The room is dark except for moonlight shining in through the window. It's still nighttime. Across the room she sees Eric, Drew, and Michael sleeping in their bunks. Marcie leans over to peer at the illuminated face of her bedside clock. Two o'clock. What did the dream mean? What was she looking for? Even now, in her familiar bed, the dream feels eerily real, and she is a little breathless, as though she had been walking briskly, or—flying? Before she can sort it all out, fatigue washes over her in a wave. She rolls over onto her side, pulling the quilt up around her shoulders, and promptly goes to sleep.

❧ Seven ❧

MARCIE SLEEPS LATE the next morning. The room is glowing with morning sunlight when she opens her eyes and slowly regains consciousness. She doesn't usually sleep in past 7:30 or 8:00, but she knows it must be later than usual, as she can hear the murmur of voices below and smell the aroma of freshly-brewed coffee. The rumpled covers on the other bunks are empty, so the boys must be up. At first she doesn't remember her dream, but when she looks over at the clock it stirs her memory and it all comes flooding back. It's been so long since she had a flying dream that she can't recall the last time. This one was particularly realistic, she thinks, but it was just a dream. But what about when she felt like she was flying on the way to the Children's Fair? She hadn't been dreaming then. Did she imagine it? Marcie has never spent much time analyzing her dreams, and since the meaning of this one isn't at all clear, she puts it out of her mind. She doesn't want to get left behind from the day's activities.

Dressing quickly in shorts and a t-shirt and sliding her feet into flip-flops, she goes downstairs to the kitchen in search of breakfast. Eric is at the counter making sandwiches.

"You missed all the bacon," he says, pointing to a plate empty except for crumbs and bacon grease. "We were going to wake you up, but Mom made us wait. It's almost ten, and we want to get out fishing." Wrapping a sandwich in foil, he asks, "Do you want ham, turkey, or bologna?"

"Ugh. I haven't even had breakfast yet. I guess I'll have ham. Is there any cheese?"

"Cheddar or Swiss?"

"Cheddar, please." Marcie pours herself a bowl of cereal and milk and takes it out to the porch. Her mom and Aunt Lucy are sitting at the table enjoying a leisurely cup of coffee and talking. Janey and Michael have toys and cars strewn all over the floor, and Michael has built a wall out of blocks around Speck and several other stuffed animals. Speck barks a greeting to Marcie, but stays good naturedly in his enclosure. Michael says, "This is my Zoo. Do you want to see it? Speck is a lion."

"Maybe after I eat. Speck is a good lion." Michael nods and goes back to playing.

"Good morning, sleepyhead. Sleep well?" asks her mom.

"Yeah." She stifles a yawn. "I'm still waking up. Where's everyone else?"

"Your dad, Uncle Mark, and Poppy are golfing, and Mamaw is—where else?—in the garden. Eric and Drew are getting ready to go fishing with Al. Are you going along too?"

"Definitely."

"I want to go fishing, Mommy!" Michael pipes up.

"We'll go fishing off the dock, honey. We don't have time before we leave to go out on the boat," replies Aunt Lucy. Janey hauls herself off the floor using Lucy's shorts and says "uppy." Lucy picks her up, sets the toddler on her lap, and continues. "I'm glad we got to see everyone yesterday. But it's never long enough." She sighs. "We'll try to come back and see you kids sometime during the week. Jill, you and Paul are leaving tonight?"

"Yes, right after the cookout at the Swyndalls'. I leave for the dig first thing in the morning. Marcie, I suggest you hurry up and get ready if you're going fishing. Drew and Eric are anxious to go. I had to stop them from waking you up. I figured you deserved to sleep in on the first day of summer." She smiles at her fondly.

"Thanks. I was really tired for some reason." *From flying*, she thinks, but sitting here at breakfast with her cousins and aunt, it seems a little ridiculous. People can't really fly. It was only a dream. She finishes her cereal and then helps Eric pack the picnic lunch. She runs upstairs to put her bathing suit on under her clothes in case they decide to go for a swim off the boat, hurries back down again and outside to the boat docks, arms loaded with beach towels and, of course, sunscreen. Eric is putting the cooler into Al's fishing boat as Marcie runs up. Drew is already in the boat. They are obviously ready to go. Al, on the other hand, is talking to one of the neighbors a few houses down and appears to be in the middle of a long story. With his free hand, the one not holding Pansy's leash, he is gesturing and pointing, and they are both laughing. His foot rests on his tackle box, and Pansy is sitting patiently on the grass beside him. When she sees Marcie, her tail thumps the ground.

"Finally!" says Eric. "At least one of you is ready. Get your life jacket, and I'll go over and get the tackle box from Al. Maybe he'll take the hint."

"What's the big hurry?"

"No hurry, really, we just want to get going before lunch! Between you and Al, we might never get out."

Al, who has finished his conversation and is walking towards them, overhears Eric's remark. "I can see you haven't converted to 'Lake Time' yet. We try never to rush at the lake." He hands Eric the tackle box and climbs into the boat. "Come on girl." He gives Pansy's leash a little tug, and she jumps in too. "Well, let's go!" he says with a laugh at the surprised look on Eric's face.

Chagrined, Eric hangs his head self-mockingly. "You're right. I shouldn't be rushing. The fish will wait." He and Marcie climb in and get settled. Al's fishing boat is a low-sided metal boat with an outboard motor on the back. It's pretty much low tech and no frills, with three bench seats, and one raised fisherman's seat towards the front. Not like the powerful speedboat her grandparents own, with its comfortable seats and drink holders. Al sits in the stern to control the engine and steer. Eric and Drew are on the middle bench with the cooler snug beneath the seat, and Marcie is in the bow with Pansy. Al starts the engine and they idle out of the cove to the main lake. As they pass by the seawall of the neighboring cottages, Drew cries out "Look, Al, the turtles!" About twenty water turtles varying in size from babies as small as saucers in a child's tea set to huge granddaddies as big around as serving platters are basking in the sun on the warm concrete. The boat isn't passing close enough to startle them into the water, so they can see them clearly. From the front of the boat Marcie sees several turtles floating submerged in the water with only their tube-like noses sticking out on the surface.

"Quick, Drew, there are some in the water over here." She points to her right and even as she speaks they start diving down into the murky depths to avoid the approaching boat.

"This has been a good spring for turtles," Al observes. "All the lake animals are flourishing. I'll bet we see some muskrats in James Bay."

"Will they have babies, too?" asks Drew.

"They just might. I saw some there last week."

"I like muskrats."

"So do I."

They pass the marker buoys indicating the end of the no-wake zone for boats, and Al opens up the engine and heads away from the shore. The nose of the boat rises up out of the water with the force of the propeller in the rear and then settles back down to plane on the surface as they get up to speed and go scudding across the waves.

The larger scow sailboats are still out on the lake from the Sunday Regatta held earlier in the morning. Several have spinnaker sails out to catch an additional breeze as they sail for home. Marcie catches sight of a bright orange sail and has a jolt of recognition. *I've seen that boat from the air,* she thinks, but then remembers it was in her dream. It's a little unsettling. She feels the way Michael described feeling about flying. Intellectually, she knows it was a dream and she didn't actually fly, but it seems so real, even now in the light of day. Is it just a coincidence that she's had the dream and imagined she was flying at the Fair? Marcie doesn't know what to think.

The smaller sunfish boats are racing now. Sunfish have one stationary sail that is usually brightly colored with large bold stripes. The sailors sit on the side of the boat with their feet in a small hollow in the center. There isn't much room; only one or two adults can fit, but you really get to experience the wind and the waves. Sunfish sailing is Marcie's favorite of the water activities—more so than the speed boat. It's like the difference between driving in a car and riding your bike. You're an active participant instead of just a passenger, and it can be both peaceful and exciting at the same time. When you catch a breeze and really get going, it's thrilling.

As they round Owen Point and the trees of James Woods come into view, Marcie has another feeling of *déjà vu*, and the urgency from her dream returns. This is really creepy! Maybe her subconscious is trying to tell her something, but she has no idea what. She must have jumped or look startled, because Al calls out, "Marcie, are you alright? You look like you've seen a ghost." She turns around and sees Al watching her intently.

"No, I'm fine. Just a little *déjà vu* when we entered the bay."

When she turns forward again, the Swyndalls' "cottage" is directly before them. The house definitely wasn't in her dream, because she would have remembered seeing it. The face the house presents to the road is impressive, but the side facing the water is really enormous and surprisingly beautiful given its size. River rock forms the lower part of the house, rising up to red painted clapboard trimmed in white. A wrap-around porch extends across the entire back of the house, and there are multiple gables, windows, and even a round cupola with a weather vane at one end.

"Wow," exclaims Eric.

"It's something else, isn't it?" says Al.

"It's big, but I like it," says Marcie. "It's not like it's the only big house on the lake." As she says this, Marcie wonders why she is defending the Swyndalls.

"Not this big!" says Eric. "It's a monster! I wonder how much time they will actually stay here. Those big summer homes are empty most of the time."

They are passing by the piers in front of the house— three piers, no less—where they see a professional ski boat, two brand new wave runners on docking stations, a pontoon boat, and a racing class E scow.

"They have a lot of toys, too," adds Eric, stating the obvious. "Those are top of the line Sea Doos!" referring to the wave runners.

"What's wrong with that?" retorts Marcie. Lately she seems to want to argue with everything Eric says. He can be so irritating.

"Who was criticizing?"

Before she can respond, a figure rises up from one of the lounge chairs on the pier, and they see it's Kaitlyn. Al honks the horn at her and they all wave. After blinking in the sunlight a few times, she recognizes them and waves her sunglasses in return as the boat passes by.

"Why do they have three docks?" asks Drew when they turn away.

"Because they can," says Eric sarcastically. "Actually, I heard Mamaw and Poppy saying that the Swyndalls were trying to discourage people from anchoring their boats in the shallows in front of the house."

"But that's a tradition!" says Drew indignantly. "They can't do that!" Drew is big on traditions and family rituals. Marcie has to agree that it doesn't seem right to take away something that used to be available to everyone.

"You're both right," says Al. "The Swyndalls can put docks into the water from the shoreline that they own, but they don't own the lake or the water in the lake, so they can't tell people not to anchor in the shallows. If you noticed, the piers didn't do much to stop people from anchoring there." They look back and see that, indeed, half a dozen large boats are anchored just past and around the docks.

"Still, it's kind of selfish of them not to share the shallows, even if they do want privacy," concludes Drew. The others don't say anything. Drew said what they all thought, too.

They negotiate the boats pulling kids on inner tubes and skis in the bay, and aim for the quieter marshy area by the shore. Once they agree on a good spot, Eric drops the anchor and Al kills the engine.

Even though Al's tackle box is full of lures and flies he has tied by hand, the kids mostly use night crawler or red wiggler worms for bait. Marcie has been fishing since she was able to walk and baiting her own hook since she was Drew's age, so putting a live, squirming worm on a hook doesn't bother her. Her friends, on the other hand, are totally grossed out by the whole process. It's bad enough to pick up the worm, but impaling it on the hook and having it ooze worm blood and squirm around is too much. Marcie usually baits the hooks when her friends visit the cottage.

They spend the next hour or so fishing and relaxing in the boat. As usual, Al and Drew catch the most fish. They each have four "keepers"—fish over six inches long—in the fish basket hanging over the side of the boat. Eric has two and Marcie doesn't have any. It's probably because she is too impatient. Fishing requires stillness and patience; two qualities she doesn't always possess. Drew can sit quietly, which is unusual for a boy his age, waiting and watching for a nibble on his line. Marcie doesn't really care about catching fish, though. She likes the peace and solitude of fishing and the companionship of Al and her brothers. At least Drew, and sometimes Eric. That peaceful feeling is interspersed today with the feeling you get that someone is looking at you and you turn around and there *is* someone looking at you—except that this time nobody is there. She keeps getting a prickly feeling on the back of her neck and turns around expecting someone in a nearby boat to be looking her way, but there aren't any boats nearby. Just the breeze moving through the trees making whispering sounds in the leaves.

As they are eating their picnic lunch, the quiet is suddenly broken when a large wave runner comes roaring up to them, executing a sharp turn in front of the boat and splashing water on them before idling around to the side and stopping.

"Thanks a lot!" yells Eric, half angry, half jokingly, as Kaitlyn laughs at them. "You got our lunch all wet."

"Well, you *are* in a boat, it's to be expected. Anyway, I'm sorry. I didn't mean to splash so much. Marcie, do you want to come over to my house for a while this afternoon? I can take you over on the wave runner."

"Are you old enough to drive the wave runner?" asks Drew. "Mamaw and Poppy say you have to be 16."

"No, I'm not 16 yet, but my parents let me take it around the bay, and I'll just be taking Marcie over to my house. What do you say, Marcie?"

Marcie looks at Al. She knows it is not only against her grandparents' rules, but also against the law for Kaitlyn to drive the wave runner. But she really wants to go. She can't tell what Al is thinking, but Eric is giving her the evil eye, which only makes her want to go that much more.

"Al, I think Mom and Dad would say it's okay since we'd just be going over to Kaitlyn's." He looks at her intently for a moment and then seems to come to a decision. He nods his head and says, "Yes, I think you should go with Kaitlyn. Just don't be gone too long. We'll be here about another hour."

"You could stay over the rest of the afternoon until the cookout if you want. Then we won't need to hurry back."

"That sounds good. Is that okay, Al?" Marcie is already climbing out of the boat onto the back of the wave runner.

"Fine with me. I'll let your parents know where you are."

"But you'll miss the rest of our fishing trip!" says Drew. "Don't you want to fish some more?"

"Oh, there will be other times, Drew. I'll see you tonight, too. Bye!" Kaitlyn starts the engine and Marcie has to raise her voice to be heard. They idle away from the boat, and then Kaitlyn takes off. Marcie looks back over her shoulder and waves. Eric is glaring at her. Drew waves back, and Al is looking thoughtful, as his hand moves slowly through the air.

❧ Eight ❧

THE GIRLS ZOOM across the water towards Owen Point and the Swyndall house. A slight outward bend of the shore obscures the house so it can't be seen from where Al and her brothers are fishing. Kaitlyn calls over her shoulder, "Why do you hang out with that old guy? It's so uncool! I bet you're glad to be rescued." Marcie feels her face flush with embarrassment and anger, and she's glad Kaitlyn can't see her. Even so, she replies, "No kidding!" enthusiastically, and then feels guilty for not defending Al. He's her friend! Once again she has mixed feelings about Kaitlyn. On the one hand, it is exciting to be riding on the wave runner without an adult and going to Kaitlyn's house, which can only be called a mansion, but she also feels guilty, like she's not only betraying Al and her family, but somehow, herself.

Kaitlyn pulls the wave runner up next to the dock instead of putting it into the docking station and, after turning off the engine, clips a rope to the front to keep it from drifting. She turns to Marcie, her eyes shining with excitement. "Do you have a bathing suit on under your clothes? You could borrow one of mine—oh, good," she continues when she sees Marcie nodding yes. "I've got a great idea. My mom's not due back home for over an hour. Why don't we go over to the sandbar for a while?"

"How will we get there?"

"The wave runner, of course."

"But you said we were just going back to your house," Marcie says uncertainly.

"What they don't know won't hurt them. Anyway, we'll just go over and see what's going on. We won't stay too long, and I'll be careful." Seeing Marcie's hesitation, she adds, "Come on! It'll be fun. You're not chicken are you?"

Actually, that's exactly how Marcie feels: Chicken. The sandbar is where the older high school and college kids go to hang out on the weekends. You can throw out your anchor and walk on the sandy bottom from boat to boat. It's like a big block party on busy weekends. She's been to the sandbar before with her family to swim, usually during the week when it's not so crowded, but never by herself. She's not even sure if she'd be allowed to go. However, the risk of being seen as "uncool" outweighs her concern about going. What's the harm anyway?

"No, I'm not chicken. You just took me by surprise. Let's do it!"

"Great! Here, take off your life jacket for a minute so you can take off your shorts and t-shirt. We won't look good at the sandbar unless we're wearing our bathing suits." She climbs onto the pier. "Hand me your stuff and I'll put it under my towel on this chair. No one will notice if they happen to come out here."

Kaitlyn climbs back onto the wave runner while Marcie refastens her life jacket. It's just one of the bunch of jackets her grandparents have in varying sizes for use by all the family and visitors who come to their house over the summer. She grew so much last winter that she can fit into one of the medium adult jackets. In contrast, Kaitlyn's jacket is a "Bodysheath," a very expensive brand which is fitted just for her. Kaitlyn unhooks the wave runner from the pier, and Marcie pushes off before Kaitlyn starts the engine.

The water splashing on Marcie's legs feels cool and refreshing as they speed along. She had gotten hot sitting at the dock in the sun in her life jacket. They can't really talk with the wind and water in their faces, so Marcie leans back and grasps the handle behind the seat to hold on. A wave runner is a lot like a motorcycle for the water. It's propelled by sucking up water and then expelling it forcefully out the back so there isn't a propeller or "prop" like a motor boat. In some ways this makes a wave runner safer because there's no risk of injury from the prop, but they can still be dangerous because they go so fast. Almost every summer they hear of a wave runner accident where someone, usually a teenager, was driving too fast and too close to another wave runner or a boat and someone is seriously injured. Marcie feels a little uneasy about riding with Kaitlyn, especially since she came at them so fast in the bay and splashed them. It's Sunday afternoon, so the lake is crowded with weekenders, and they have to be careful to avoid other water craft. Since the wave runner can maneuver the most easily, they must give the right of way to speed boats and sailboats, which are the least maneuverable. Marcie is relieved that Kaitlyn is giving wide berth to other vehicles and not going too fast.

They reach the sandbar, and Kaitlyn slows to idle speed. "Let's cruise around a bit and see who's here," she says over her shoulder. She steers them around the boats, careful to avoid anchor lines and people floating on rafts and noodles. It's a clear, sunny day without too much wind, and there are at least 40 boats sitting at anchor, all pointing into the current as the anchors keep them from drifting away. Marcie suddenly realizes that she might see someone she knows, and then what'll she do? Hide? Pretend not to see them? She'd be in for it then. It would not be pretty if someone mentioned seeing her at the sandbar to her parents or grandparents. She keeps close behind Kaitlyn, hoping that no one recognizes her. Quite a few families are here, but also a lot of teenagers, and Marcie notices that many of them are drinking beer.

Whispering over her shoulder, Kaitlyn says, "Look—over there on that red ski boat. That's my brother, Kyle, and his friends. Let's go over and say hi." Not waiting for an answer, she steers toward the boat and calls out "Kyle!" A tall blond boy wearing blue bathing trunks covered in white stars looks up.

"Kaitlyn? What're you doing here?" He shades his eyes from the sun with his hand.

"Marcie and I just came out to see what was going on." Marcie smiles faintly and gives a little wave with her fingers that she hopes looks nonchalant. The other three boys on the boat are looking down on them, and somehow she feels like a little kid sitting behind Kaitlyn. She is glad to see that they are drinking sodas and not beer.

"Mom know you're here and on the wave runner?"

"Of course not!"

"Well, you'd better head back. Now that I'm in on it, I'll get blamed if anything happens." Glancing at Marcie, he says, "Is this the friend who is going to race with us?"

"Yes, Marcie Horton. Her family's coming for dinner tonight."

"Hey," he says, and then, motioning to a boy in red swim trunks with reflective sunglasses, he adds, "This is Conner Phelps. He's our fourth. Conner—Kaitlyn and Marcie."

Conner gives them a salute, "Nice to meet you ladies."

71

Kaitlyn says hi, and Marcie smiles back. She's mortified to realize that she is blushing. She can feel the heat rising up her neck out of her life jacket and knows it is not because she's hot.

"Well, we better get back before Mom does. Maybe we can figure out what days to practice later tonight."

The boys turn back to whatever they were doing. After they get out of earshot, Marcie asks, "How old is your brother?"

"Seventeen. He'll be a senior in high school this year. Aren't his friends cute? I've never met Conner before, but he's a hottie!"

"Yeah!" replies Marcie, who had noticed the boys' tanned, muscled chests and attractive good looks, but it had made her feel more uncomfortable than actually interested. As far as she is concerned, they are way out of her league.

๛ Nine ๛

MARCIE IS RELIEVED when they get back to Kaitlyn's house without incident. No one is visible on the docks or at the back of the house as they approach.

"Awesome!" Kaitlyn exclaims. "The coast is clear. We'll tie up the Sea-Doo and go inside for a snack. I'm starving."

"Sounds good to me!" Marcie unsnaps her life jacket and leaves it on a chair to dry. She follows Kaitlyn up to the house. "So Kyle won't tell on you? I know Eric would probably rat on me."

"No way—I have too much dirt on him. Anyway, he's older and been through it all before, so I guess he doesn't care as much. As long as he isn't held responsible."

They cross the patio, climb two steps onto the back porch and enter the kitchen through sliding glass doors. It's an enormous room with gleaming stainless steel appliances and a huge center island. Six bar stools line one side of the island. It hardly looks used. *Definitely not much cooking going on here*, thinks Marcie. No food or plates are on the counter tops and nothing looks out of place. Almost like a picture in a magazine. Kaitlyn disappears through a door to what must be the pantry because she emerges carrying boxes of cookies and fruit snacks and a bag of chips. Behind her, Marcie can see shelves loaded with canned goods and food in boxes.

"The mother lode!" Kaitlyn says, smiling as she puts the food down on the island. "Help yourself. There's also a bowl of fruit on the counter. Do you want a soda or lemonade?"

"Lemonade, please."

She takes two tumblers from a cabinet, pours lemonade from a pitcher in the fridge and places them on the counter. They sit down at the island and start munching.

"So what kinds of stuff do you usually do when you're up here?" Kaitlyn asks.

"Oh, there's lots to do. We go fishing and sailing and swim in the cove. Of course, we go tubing and skiing on the speed boat, too." They rarely have potato chips at home, so she opens that bag first. "Sometimes we play miniature golf at Watson Lake or go into town for ice cream. The best part of being at the lake, though, is just hanging out and relaxing and not having to do anything."

"Hmm . . . sounds fun." Kaitlyn says this in a way that makes it clear that it doesn't sound fun. "Do you belong to the Yacht Club?" She opens her second package of fruit snacks.

"No, I've never been."

"We should go sometime—my parents belong. Swimming in the pool is much nicer than the lake. All that seaweed—ick."

"Yeah, I'd like to go." Marcie feels a little bit like she is being absorbed into Kaitlyn's world, doing all these things she has never done before. She never wanted to until now. It's all pretty exciting, but she feels somewhat off balance—not quite herself.

They decide to go up to Kaitlyn's room for a while, and Marcie feels a pang of envy as she enters the room. It's bigger than her room at home and is furnished with a four-poster canopy bed, an armchair and footstool, and Kaitlyn has her own private bathroom. Everything matches—the curtains, bedding, towels, and carpet—like it was all purchased at the same time. Which it probably was. They did just move in this summer.

"Wow!" she says admiringly. "You have a great room. Is your room at home this nice?"

"Thanks. Do you like the flip flop theme?" She gestures to the bedspread where the recurring pattern of sandals in pastel shades of pink and orange appears. "My mom and I found all the bedding and towels on the Internet. We coordinated everything. It's perfect for the lake, don't you think? My room at home is okay, but now I want to redecorate it, too! I saw some really great stuff in this magazine. Here, I'll show you." Kaitlyn grabs a magazine from her dresser and plops down on the bed, motioning for Marcie to join her. They look through magazines and catalogues picking out things they like, reading articles and giving each other quizzes to find out "What Kind of Friend are You?"

They are in the middle of reading an article about planning a slumber party when Mrs. Swyndall pops her head into the doorway. "Kaitlyn—Oh, hello, Marcie. I didn't know you were here."

"Hi, Mrs. Swyndall." Marcie looks up from her magazine and feels her heart start pounding anxiously as she has the irrational thought that somehow Mrs. Swyndall will know that they took the wave runner to the sand bar. She is about to say more, but Kaitlyn quickly jumps in and says, "I saw Marcie and her brothers go into James Bay to go fishing earlier today, so I picked her up on the wave runner and brought her over here. I hope that was okay." She smiles innocently at her mom.

"Oh, sure, no problem. As long as you stay in the bay."

"I know, Mom," Kaitlyn says calmly. Marcie can feel herself flush guiltily. She's not used to deceiving adults, and not sure how she feels about it.

"Well, I just got back from the store and I could use some help unpacking the food and setting up for the barbeque. Why don't you two get dressed and come down to give me a hand?"

Marcie realizes she is still wearing her bathing suit and that she left her clothes on the dock. "I'll just run down to the dock to get my clothes. My suit is dry so I can put them on over it."

Kaitlyn walks over to the door and checks the hallway. Certain that her mom has left, she claps her hands gleefully and says, "Did you see how I handled that? Take it from the pro, it's always best to be right up front with information, so they don't think you're hiding anything. Just don't blow it when you see Kyle." She points a scolding finger at Marcie. "Remember, you haven't met him yet."

"Got it," replies Marcie with a snap of her fingers and more confidence than she feels. She thinks, *I could be an actress, I feel like I'm playing the part of someone else!* "Well, I'll be back in a few."

She decides to go down the front staircase—yes, there are two stairways—so she can see more of the house. The two doors she passes in the upstairs hallway are obviously guest bedrooms—attractive, but impersonal. The family's bedrooms are at the back of the house, to take in the lake views. On her way through the downstairs front entry she hears the muffled sound of someone talking. She doesn't think about why she decides to follow the sound of the voice, but it does seem that something is compelling her to do it. She walks silently across the geometrically patterned hall rug in nautical shades of red, white, and blue, and, feeling a little strange in her bathing suit, approaches the room where voices can be heard. The door is slightly ajar and she pauses to listen where she can just barely see inside but won't be seen herself.

Mr. Swyndall is sitting at his desk with his back to her. He is using the speaker phone and Marcie can hear the person on the other end of the line speaking. A man's voice is saying "Yes . . . we have the permits all in place. We don't need to get special approval since it's private property and the zoning is all taken care of."

"Great. We want to move ahead quickly on this to avoid interference from anyone. It should be presented as a public area with walking and biking paths. Everyone will go for that. The gated community is secondary until we're too far into the project for objections to stick." Mr. Swyndall leans back in his chair and puts his hands behind his head. "Then we can start selling building lots."

"It's all taken care of," the disembodied voice on the phone says confidently. "James Woods Park is the name we'll be using at first. It won't be James Woods Estates until we're ready to start building houses."

James Woods Estates! Building houses! So her fears from last night were real. Mr. Swyndall is planning to develop James Woods, and he's not being entirely up front about what he's doing. She wonders how much Al really knows about this. He seemed unsatisfied with Mr. Swyndall's answers last night, but he didn't press it too much. Maybe he was being polite. Marcie knows she should move away from the door before she's caught eavesdropping, but she feels rooted to the spot. It would be difficult to explain what she is doing hanging out in the hallway in her bathing suit.

"Alright, then. Keep me posted," Mr. Swyndall says. "We'll talk on Monday." He leans over the desk and presses a button on the phone to hang up.

Oh, no! Marcie thinks. He's hanging up. *Quick, back to the entry.* Her paralysis transformed to action, Marcie swiftly and silently pads in her bare feet back to the entryway. Once there, she sees a doorway that leads to the kitchen and the back of the house and hurries towards it. She is slightly out of breath from shock and exertion when she enters the kitchen. Mrs. Swyndall is unpacking grocery bags.

"I left my clothes outside on the dock," she says with a wave. "I'll just get dressed and we'll be down to help you get ready." She has a fleeting and irrational thought about trying out for the next school play. She really is good at this. Especially since all the while her mind is whirling with thoughts—*Oh my gosh, what am I going to do? How can I stop this, and who will believe me anyway?*

ᴓ Ten ᴓ

MARCIE SPENDS THE rest of the afternoon and evening in a daze. Her thoughts keep distracting her by going back to the conversation she overheard. She and Kaitlyn get dressed and help Mrs. Swyndall set up for the party, but Marcie isn't paying attention to what she is doing and almost drops a platter of watermelon before she gets herself in hand. When her parents and brothers arrive with her grandparents in tow, there isn't any opportunity for her to talk with them alone about what she found out. She's practically bursting with her knowledge, and she's so worried that she'll confront Mr. Swyndall in front of everyone that she tries to stay completely away from him. Not that it's too difficult. He is standing around the grill with the other men and not paying much attention to the girls.

One part of the evening stands out clearly in her mind. When Kyle and Conner come back from the sandbar and introductions are made all around, Kaitlyn announces, "You are looking at the future winning team of the July 4th Regatta!" Her hand sweeps across Kyle, Conner, Marcie, and herself, who all happen to be standing together by the drinks cooler. A brief silence follows that seems to last a lot longer than a few seconds to Marcie. Then everyone exhibits slightly different reactions to the news. Her parents and the Swyndalls are pleased at the idea. The moms particularly so, since they suggested that they do some sailing together in the first place.

"Oh, that'll be fun, Marce. You've always wanted to compete in the races!" says her mom. Her dad is looking a little warily at Kyle and Conner, probably thinking the same thing as Marcie had at the sand bar—that they are too old for her, but he says, "The Regatta Champions, huh? Looks like the Boat Company team will have some competition this year, Eric." He nudges Eric in the ribs.

Eric's surprise is immediately evident on his face. His mouth hangs slightly open and his eyes are wide, but he quickly regains his composure. Raising one eyebrow and tilting his head to one side, he says, "I wouldn't be too confident about winning. There are a lot of good teams competing." He pauses and adds, "Anyway, we're ready… Bring it on!"

Mr. Swyndall says, "So, Eric, you're on the Boat Company team? I heard there was a bit of a rivalry with the Yacht Club. That'll be a great way to break in the new E scow. A little healthy competition!" He thumps Kyle on the back.

"Yeah, we're up for it." Kyle nods in Eric's direction acknowledging the challenge. Turning to Marcie, Kaitlyn, and Conner he says, "How do Tuesday and Thursday look for us to practice? Are you guys free? About 10 a.m. should be a good time for the wind." They all agree to meet at the Swyndalls' on Tuesday. Then, in addition to avoiding Mr. Swyndall, Marcie also avoids Eric for the rest of the evening. That doesn't stop him from glowering at her from across the room, though.

IN THE VAN on the way back to Mamaw and Poppy's, they barely pull out of the driveway before Marcie blurts out, "Al was right! Mr. Swyndall is planning to build a gated community in James Woods! I overheard him talking to someone on the phone about acting to everyone like they were going to develop the land into a public park, but they are really planning to make it into private estates! What are we going to do? He can't do that to James Woods. It's our special place." It all comes out in a rush and when she pauses for breath, her dad says, "Whoa! Slow down a minute. Now what exactly did you hear?"

She tells them about overhearing the conversation and what was said and adds, "We have to stop him!"

"Oh, that's terrible," says Mamaw. "Those woods are some of the only undeveloped land left on the lake. Sometimes when I walk there, I almost feel like I'm in a sacred place."

"It is his land, Marce. He said he already has all the permits, too," says Poppy resignedly. "I'm not sure there is much we can do."

"Your mother and I are in a difficult position, honey," says her dad, sighing. "First of all, we're going home tonight, and your mom is heading to Utah in the morning, so we won't even be around, and secondly, Mr. Swyndall is technically our boss as president of the university. We have to be careful about how we handle this."

Marcie can't believe what she's hearing. "You're not all going to give up without trying are you?" she cries. "This is our lake too, and we should fight for it. He's a Laker and all the people who buy the houses will be Lakers. They don't care about the lake the same way we do. They won't even live here full time. It's just an investment for them. We have to do something!"

They are all quiet for a moment, lost in their thoughts, and then Marcie's mom says, "Perhaps there's something about the land that would prevent them from developing it. It is pretty marshy in the bay, maybe it's wetlands or something."

"Or a wildlife sanctuary!" says Eric excitedly.

They arrive at the cottage, and her dad turns off the engine. For a moment they all just sit in the van. Then her dad says, "Well, kids, your mom and I have to hit the road now if we're going to get home at a decent hour." He turns around to face Marcie. "It doesn't look like we're going to be in a position to offer much help on this, but there may be some things that you can do. Al might want to be involved." He opens the door of the van and gets out. "Jill, I'll bring our bags out and load up the car." They are taking Mamaw and Poppy's car and leaving the van for them to use.

"Thanks. Here, kids, give me a hug goodbye," her mom says. "I won't see you for a couple weeks. Not until the Fourth." They all get out of the van and say goodbye. Their dad loads up the car and they drive away. The kids stand on the driveway, waving until the car turns the corner out of sight. Drew and her grandparents start to go into the house, but Eric says to Marcie, "Let's go find Al and tell him what you heard. He may be able to help."

"We're going over to Al's house for a while," Eric calls to Mamaw and Poppy.

Since the Summer Solstice is only a few days away, the days are long and there is still plenty of daylight left as they walk over the lawn and along the sea wall towards Al's house, which sits closer to the water than their cottage. They are silent until they reach the water, and then Eric says, "Don't think I've forgotten about the Regatta.

What're you thinking of, crewing for a Laker team? They're just using you to win, you know."

"Well, I want to win too," Marcie replies indignantly. "And who says it's not me who's using them? I can't crew for the Boat Company team, and there aren't any other teams asking me. And, it's really none of your business."

"Well, just watch yourself. You know as well as I do that Kaitlyn hangs out with the popular crowd. They can be fickle friends. One day you're 'in' and the next day you're 'out.' Who needs friends like that?"

"Have a little faith in me, why don't you? It's not like I'm trying to be part of that crowd—it's just a sailboat race. Anyway, Kaitlyn's not like all the rest of them. She's genuinely nice." Even as she says this, though, Marcie knows it's not entirely true, judging by some of Kaitlyn's behavior that day.

"I guess I'm just surprised you were taken in so easily by the Swyndalls and all their stuff. They're not really our type."

Marcie heaves an exasperated sigh, but doesn't say any more. They've reached Al's back porch, and she can see him sitting on the swing with Pansy at his feet.

"Hey there, you two! I could use some company. Come for some candy?"

"No, I mean, yes, we'd love some candy, but we really came to tell you that you were right about Mr. Swyndall.

He is planning to develop James Woods into houses. I heard him talking to someone on the phone about it at their house," Marcie says, as she and Eric sit down in the rocking chairs across from Al.

"I see," he says grimly. "What exactly did you hear?"

For the second time, Marcie recounts the conversation she overheard. Al closes his eyes and listens, absently stroking Pansy's head, his head nodding slightly as if in confirmation.

"I thought as much. A friend at the zoning commission said they were developing the land into a park area, but he implied that there was more to it than that, without actually telling me anything."

"We've got to try to stop it, Al," says Eric. "What can we do? Poppy thinks that we can't do anything if Swyndall already has the permits in place, and Mom and Dad are hesitant to help because Mr. Swyndall is president of the university."

"Yes, I can see how that would be tricky for them. Hmm . . . I'm not sure what we can do—yet. Let's make a visit to the Zoning Commission tomorrow. I believe those permits are a matter of public record. Perhaps my friend over there can tell us our options now that we know what's really going on."

"Mom suggested that it might be considered wetlands. Aren't those protected? Also, since Mr. Swyndall's trying to hide what they're really doing, he must think people won't like it. We could get a petition going!"

"Those are good ideas. Why don't you two come by first thing tomorrow morning? Now, I need to get these old bones inside." Twilight has fallen since they arrived, and a pearly grey light bathes the cove. A light breeze causes the flags hanging on nearly every pier to clang gently against the flag poles. Al rises slowly from the swing using his cane for support and Pansy jumps down beside him. "Don't come by before 9 a.m., though. They don't open till then, and I don't want to get up any earlier. See you in the morning." He walks stiffly to the screen door and lets it bang shut behind him.

❧ Eleven ❧

MAMAW AND MARCIE are getting out of the van at the farmer's market when one of those army-type sports utility vehicles pulls into the spot next to them. The front of the truck is as tall as Marcie's shoulder, and the engine roars slightly before the driver turns it off. Startled, Speck starts barking wildly, so Mamaw picks him up and says, "They scare me too! Don't worry—I won't let the Monster truck get you."

The two of them were up early, so they decided to make a visit to Yoder's Market while the selection is still good. The market is run by a Mennonite family and is very popular with the Lakers, so the produce goes fast. In fact, it's rather busy already and it's only 8:30 in the morning.

"Why do people buy those trucks? They can't be very comfortable, and Mom and Dad say they're gas guzzlers," Marcie says while selecting strawberries from the bins set up in rows under the big yellow market tent and then collecting them in cardboard pint containers.

"My theory is that people are always striving for bigger and better things, thinking that it will make them happy or feel more important. It may work at first, but then the feeling wears off and they have to get something else—like the biggest truck they can buy. It's a never-ending cycle because there's always something else bigger and better." She surveys the pints they have filled. "Is this enough?"

"Let's get a few more. Maybe you could make short-cake again—it was great—and Drew likes them with cereal, too." She pauses contemplatively, then asks, "Mamaw, what's so wrong with wanting to have things? You have a nice house, and I like getting new things."

"Well, I certainly can't claim to be immune to nice things, but I don't think it is really the things that cause the problem, it's more the importance we place on them. After all, it's just stuff." They finish selecting their fruits and vegetables and wait in line to pay. A display of homemade preserves, pie fillings, and apple butter is on the counter. Behind the counter, the oldest daughters of the Yoder family are weighing packages and totaling up orders. *They probably made all the preserves themselves last fall*, thinks Marcie. The older boys are helping their father unload the truck at the back of the tent. The Mennonite religion allows them to drive cars and use electricity, unlike Amish families who don't use either, but like the Amish, they choose to live in a simpler, more old-fashioned way. They wear plain clothing without zippers and usually make a living as farmers or shop owners, or in a trade such as carpentry. A fairly large community of Amish and Mennonite families lives in northern Indiana, and you often see horse-drawn Amish buggies driven by black-clad bearded men going along the side of the road.

When it is their turn to pay, Rachel Yoder, who's a few years older than Marcie, checks them out. She is dressed simply in a light blue cotton dress. Her hair is pinned up into a bun and covered by a white cap with the string ties dangling down her back. "How's your mother, Rachel? I haven't seen her in a while," asks Mamaw.

"Very well, thank you," replies Rachel, smiling. "She's home today with the youngest since they're out of school. Hello, Marcie! Are you finished with school, too?" Her grey-blue eyes gaze inquiringly at Marcie, and not for the first time, Marcie is taken by her poise and serenity. Rachel doesn't seem to have many insecurities. She's always pleasant and smiling and working hard. Like the rest of her family, she exudes health and contentment. Although Marcie wouldn't want to live they way they do, given her conversation with Mamaw, she finds herself wondering about whether simpler might be better in some ways.

"Yes, Friday was the last day. My brothers and I are staying with Mamaw and Poppy for a few weeks."

"Lucky you!" Rachel exclaims without any real envy. "I guess I'll be seeing you again, then." She finishes weighing and bagging their purchases, makes change for Mamaw, and turns to the next customer with a friendly smile.

Back in the van, Marcie rolls down her window so Speck can put his head out as they drive. She is still thinking about Rachel and her family, and she can't help comparing them to Kaitlyn and the Swyndalls. The Swyndalls have so much, but to Marcie, there's a hollow feeling to it, like trying to fill a bottomless pit. The thing is, she's not immune to the allure of nice things either, and finds herself both drawn to and repelled by the Swyndalls. The Yoders, although far from poor, make do with much less. Marcie isn't really sure if the Yoders are happier than the Swyndalls, it just seems like they might be. Maybe she's romanticizing their way of life. Farming is really hard, never-ending work, and the Amish do everything without modern conveniences like tractors and dishwashers. She is reminded of the conversation with her mom about people not being in touch with the natural world anymore. As farmers, the Yoders must live with the rhythm of nature and the changing seasons. If they don't take care of the land, it won't take care of them.

Marcie thinks about James Woods and how much they will all miss its natural setting and the wildlife that lives there and in the shallows of the bay. If it is turned into a gated housing development where wealthy people can build exclusive vacation homes, something special will be lost forever.

೧ Twelve ೧

THE BACK DOOR to Al's cottage is closed, which is unusual if he's at home. Eric checks his watch and says, "It's 9:15. Maybe he's not home. He's always up by now and he told us to come over after nine. Should we knock?"

"Yeah, I think we should," Marcie replies, and gives the screen door three sharp raps with her knuckles. They hear Al call out faintly, "Just a minute." They glance at each other, and Marcie gives a little shrug as if to say 'I don't know any more that you do.' When Al finally does open the door, they are surprised to see he's still wearing his pajamas and bathrobe. Pansy is hugging very close to his side.

"Hi, kids," he says, running a hand through his sparse hair to smooth it down. "I don't think I can make our outing just yet. I had a rough night, and I think I'll just putter around this morning. How about going after lunch?"

"Are you sick? Is there anything we can do?" Marcie asks, concerned.

"No, not sick, just old," says Al, making light of it. "I'll be better in a little bit. Pansy's taking good care of me." He fondles her ears. "In fact, she won't leave me alone!" He turns to go back into the house. "I'll be out after lunch, and then we'll go."

"Okay," Eric says. "I hope you feel better." They walk back to the cottage.

In the kitchen, Mamaw is just finishing putting away the groceries from the market. Marcie sits down on a stool, "Mamaw, we just went over to Al's and he wasn't even dressed yet. He said he had a bad night. Is something wrong?"

"I don't know if he's actually ill, but he does seem to be short of breath occasionally. He doesn't like to talk about it. It could just be old age. I wouldn't worry too much about it."

But Marcie is worried. It's hard to see the people you love getting older and more feeble. She's known Al all her life. Now she feels at loose ends since their plans have changed. Eric took Drew and went to shoot baskets with the boy next door, but that's not really her thing. Maybe she'll take the sunfish out for a sail. It will be the first of the season and will give her some time alone to think. "I'm going to take the sunfish out for a bit," she says, as she slides off the stool to the floor.

"That's a good idea. Poppy got it all ready for you last week. It's rigged and ready to go at the dock." She wipes her hands on a dish towel. "Have fun."

After changing into her suit and getting a life jacket out of the shed, Marcie is quickly down at the dock unsnapping the cover on the sail boat. The mast, sail, and boom are lying across the top of the boat, and inside the tiny cockpit are the centerboard, rudder, and a paddle. The boat is only 14 feet long and is comfortable for one sailor but a bit tight for two. She attaches the rudder to the stern of the boat and, while standing on the dock, slips the mast into the socket in the bow of the boat. The metal boom, which anchors the bottom edge of the sail, is attached to the mast with a metal ring and extends out toward the stern or back of the boat. Marcie climbs on board and arranges the boom and sail on the deck in front of her. She will paddle out past the marker buoys a ways to avoid getting blown back to shore or encountering too many boats before raising the sail.

Fortunately, it isn't too wavy, so she easily maneuvers the light craft out past the boat traffic. Before raising the sail, she checks to make sure she has the main sheet loosely cleated to the boat so it doesn't blow out of her reach if the sail catches the wind. The main sheet is the rope, or line in sailing terms, that controls the mainsail via the boom. On the sunfish it is the only line on the boat, and

Marcie will sail with the tiller and the main sheet. Then she inserts the center board through a slit in the bottom of the boat so it protrudes underneath to provide stability. She checks to see that there are no boats around and then hoists the sail to the top of the mast and fastens the rope to a cleat on the deck. It catches the breeze immediately and Marcie pulls in the line until the sail is full and she can feel the boat start to glide through the water. She's sailing!

It is quiet on the boat, but there are still plenty of sounds. The thump of the hull as it hits and slices through each wave, the splash of the water falling away from the sides of the boat, the cawing of the gulls, and the rush of the wind. Up close you can see that the water isn't one solid color, but a constantly changing, moving pattern of shadow and light, dark green, pale green, silver and white. In the distance she can hear speed boats and people laughing, and although she is alone, she's not lonely.

She lets the wind take her with no particular destination or course in mind. It is coming over the starboard or right side of the boat. When she gets too close to boat traffic she decides to change direction and come about so the wind is coming over the port side of the boat and she is going back in the opposite direction. She pushes the tiller board to the right to turn the bow of the boat left, and at just the right moment she swings the boom across the boat, ducks underneath it, moves her position to the opposite side, pulling in the main sheet to fill the sail with wind. She traverses across the water this way in a series of zig zags. It's another hot day, but the deck is only a few inches off the water, so Marcie is regularly splashed with cool spray coming off the hull of the boat. The rhythm of sailing casts its spell over her, and she is completely immersed in experiencing the wind, water, and motion of the boat. She doesn't realize that she has sailed into James Bay until she looks up and sees the trees of James Woods across the water.

Surprised, Marcie thinks, *maybe I unconsciously headed in this direction when I thought I was just sailing aimlessly.* She realizes that this is the second time she's been drawn to James Bay since arriving at the cottage. The first time was in her dream, and now it happened while she was totally focused on sailing. And then yesterday while they were fishing, she kept having those funny feelings of someone watching her. Okay, she thinks, why not just go with it? She sails further across the bay to the reeds in front of the woods. Since it's Monday morning there isn't much boat traffic, just a few fishing boats. She lowers the sail and folds it on the deck with the boom. *Now what? Maybe I should sit here quietly and see what happens.* She leans back against the mast, closes her eyes, and tries to empty her mind. Nothing happens at first, but after a few minutes she feels herself becoming more relaxed and a little drowsy. Her thoughts are floating in and out. Then, instead of her thoughts, she starts seeing images. At first they are hazy and unclear. Gradually, she sees people dressed in leather tunic-like clothing, maybe animal skins, performing a sort of ceremony. They are sitting on a semi-circular raised area in a clearing by the shore of a lake surrounded by trees on three sides. She sees earthenware pots and smoke gently rising from a fire in the center of the grouping. Marcie gets a sense that this is a religious or spiritual ceremony. One person in particular catches her attention. A girl about Marcie's age is on the edge of the group. Her long dark hair is fastened with a leather cord at the back of her neck and a copper-colored bracelet encircles the upper part of her slender arm. She's not actually looking at Marcie, but somehow Marcie feels like the girl is aware of her. Then the girl turns and looks directly at Marcie as though she can see her. Marcie feels a frisson of recognition. Is it the girl from the maze and the mirror? They make what feels like eye contact, and Marcie senses the girl trying to communicate with Marcie through her thoughts.

The roar of an engine shatters the calm and pulls Marcie out of her semi-dream state. She opens her eyes and sees the fishing boat that had been anchored nearby moving away. She is still partly in her dream-like state and has a vivid picture of the scene in her mind. The girl was trying to tell her something. Had she also tried to communicate with her through her dream? Could she be the same girl from the maze? Just now she got a sense of some message. Something about James Bay and James Woods, but what? She tries to regain the image, but it is gone. She looks out at James Woods and sees only trees.

What is it all about? she wonders. They were obviously an ancient people, judging by their clothing and tools. Why did she see those images? How could it be that she saw them? And most importantly, how is it that she felt she could communicate with the girl? Is she imagining things?

It certainly felt real. As real as sitting in the boat right now. Just like her dream from the other night. Is this girl from an ancient time trying to help her somehow? Or maybe it is her overactive imagination trying to find a solution to the problem of James Woods Estates. The people in her vision were seated on a low circular mound near the shore of what Marcie assumed was Lake Pappakeechee. It is all somewhat unsettling and brings more questions than answers.

She shakes her head to remove the last remnants of her daydream, and hoists the sail for the trip back home. When she reaches her grandparents' dock, she is still no closer to making sense of it all, but she knows that somehow what she is experiencing is real. Her sixth sense is picking up something about these people. She doesn't seem to be able to control it or make sense of it yet.

She can only hope and believe that things will add up soon.

❧ Thirteen ❧

THAT AFTERNOON, AL drives Eric and Marcie to the Department of Planning and Development in town in his ancient wide-track Pontiac sedan. Al is a careful driver—perhaps too careful. He drives so slowly he is almost a menace to the other drivers by disrupting the normal flow of traffic. Marcie notices several cars stop abruptly to avoid him or pull out to try to pass his slow-moving vehicle. There are a couple of near misses to which Al is oblivious, but they get there without an accident. Inside the building, they approach a long counter with a middle-aged man dressed in khakis and a blue button-down shirt seated at a desk just beyond it. Rows and rows of filing cabinets fill the room. He sees them come in and rises, reaching across the counter to shake Al's hand.

"Hello, Al, how've you been? Hey, kids," he says as they shake hands.

"I can't complain, Bob. These bones have a lot of mileage on them, but I'm holding up pretty well. How're things with you?"

"'Bout the same. Been doing much fishing?"

"Yup. Caught some nice blue gills over off the south shore by the new condos the other day. They were biting good."

Listening to this exchange, Marcie wonders how long it will take for Al to get down to business and ask about the zoning permits for James Woods. She rolls her eyes at Eric, but he shrugs, seeming content to let the men go through the social pleasantries. After being reprimanded for being impatient before they went fishing the other day, he must have gotten on Lake Time. Marcie taps her fingers on the counter in an effort to speed things up.

"I'll have to try that spot. What brings you by today?"

"We've been hearing some rumors about development plans for James Woods. Don Swyndall says they're planning to develop it into a nature park, but we heard there might be more to it than that. Do you know anything about it?"

"Actually, I was hoping someone would come around asking about it. I tried to give you some hints the last time I saw you. As a commission employee, I can't really comment or take action on the permits we issue, but the permits are a matter of public record. This one hits a little too close to home. I played in James Woods as a child, and so did my children. I hope it will still be around for my grandchildren to play there." He turns to the nearest filing cabinet, opens a drawer and searches for a file.

"I remembered what you said the other day and tried to pin Swyndall down when I saw him at the Hortons' house, but he was very vague about his plans."

"We heard they are planning to build a gated community of Estate Homes—in James Woods," Marcie says indignantly.

"What can we do to stop them?" asks Eric.

Bob finds the file he is looking for. "Building and development permits are a matter of public record." He lays the file open on the counter. "The initial plans do call for development of a park with walking and biking trails and picnic areas with very little disturbance to the existing forest. Then in stage two, which is carefully buried in the permit, development of a large and exclusive gated community is planned—James Woods Estates." He pauses and looks at Eric. "I'm not sure what we can do to stop them. James Woods is privately owned and only needed minor rezoning to allow for multiple homes. The public hearing about the rezoning took place early this spring, and no opposition was voiced. Of course, no one really knew about the hearing either."

"What about wetlands or wildlife habitats? It's really marshy there, and the woods are full of birds and animals.

The lagoons back home are protected because it's a wetland area," says Eric hopefully.

"That's not really my area of specialty. You'd need to contact the Department of Natural Resources, but I do know that there are ways around the wetlands issue. There are specific criteria that need to be met to qualify as wetlands, and only a small portion of the site is marshy anyway. It's mostly woods. I would think the Lake Area Conservation Society would have already identified it as wetlands if it qualified."

"So what course of action can we take?" asks Al.

"You could try to get public opinion against it. I've seen that stop development before."

"You mean start a petition or something?" asks Marcie.

"Yes, a petition could work. Right now, no one knows what he's really planning. If you raised public awareness, maybe people would oppose it. That kind of pressure can work, but Swyndall still can do what he wants to with the land even in the face of public opposition."

"I could get a petition together and make posters," says Eric enthusiastically. "We could go door to door and get signatures."

"I don't want to get your hopes up about a petition, but it's worth a try. Really, the best way to stop any development in James Woods is to get it classified as a cultural or historical resource. Cultural Resources are actually owned by the state even if they are on private land. They are much more strongly protected than wetlands or wildlife."

"What's a cultural resource?" asks Eric.

"Anything that is of historical significance to Indiana, like a pioneer settlement—"

"Or an Indian ceremonial site?" says Marcie quietly.

"Exactly, but there isn't any evidence of Native American sites around Pappakeechee," he shrugs.

Al turns toward the door and gestures to Eric with his cane. "I guess you should get to work on your petition. That seems like the best place to start. We'll just have to see what develops from the other possibilities. Thanks for your help, Bob."

"Good luck. You know I'm on your side."

As they walk down the stairs in front of the building, Marcie says, "I wish Mom were here. She'd know more about Cultural Resources. I don't think we can reach her very easily in the middle of the desert." *I wish I could talk to her about these strange things that are happening, too*, she thinks. "Sara's dad is some sort of environmental attorney. Maybe he can help us stop the development."

"That's a great idea!" says Eric. "He probably knows some pretty high-powered people. People with a different agenda than Mr. Swyndall."

"I'll call Sara tonight and see if I can talk to her Dad. I don't think she leaves for tennis camp until Wednesday."

They slam the car doors and Al carefully edges out of the parking lot.

SARA'S MOM ANSWERS the phone in her sing-song accent, and Marcie can hear the jingling of her silver bracelets in the background. She waited until evening to call so there would be a better chance of Sara's dad being home. "Hello, Mrs. Clements, it's Marcie. Is Sara home?"

"Oh, hello, Marcie. I hope you are enjoying the lake with your grandparents. Sara is upstairs packing for camp. I will get her for you."

"Thank you," replies Marcie. Sara's mom speaks a bit formally, and it makes Marcie want to be polite in return. As she waits for Sara to come on the line, she pictures the Clements' home in her mind. It is a very large house with gleaming hardwood floors and polished woodwork, but it is primarily a family home and it feels comfortable and lived in. She knows that Sara's family is wealthy, but Marcie realizes that she doesn't think much about it. They don't put a lot of emphasis on it somehow.

"Marcie!" Sara exclaims when she gets on the phone. "Boy, has it been dead around here. I'm even looking forward to camp. How're things at the cottage?"

"Good. The water's warm and we've already been swimming and sailing, and of course, fishing. There's actually a really bad thing happening, though. Do you remember James Bay and James Woods from when you were up here? The area where we usually go to water ski?"

"I think so—with all the trees and cattails down by the water?"

"Right. Well, the woods are on Kaitlyn Swyndall's family property, and I overheard Mr. Swyndall saying he is going to develop it into a gated community of estate houses."

"No way! That's a really cool place."

"I thought maybe your dad might be able to help or have some suggestions for what we could do."

"So you really didn't want to talk to me at all," Sara exclaims with mock indignation. "Seriously, I'm sure he'll talk with you. I think he's in his office downstairs. Hang on a sec."

After a few moments, Sara's dad gets on the phone. "Hello, Marcie. Sara gave me some details, but why don't you fill me in on what is going on, and I'll see what I can do to help."

Marcie knows Sara's dad from seeing him over at their house, but she hasn't spent a lot of time in conversation with him. He seems disconcertingly professional now, on the phone, so she is a little nervous as she explains about James Woods, the secretive development plans of Mr. Swyndall, and their visit to the Zoning Commission that afternoon. "We hoped that you might have some suggestions for how we can stop the development. My brother, Eric, is starting a petition and we wondered if maybe the property could be declared a wetlands or wildlife habitat," she finishes a bit hesitantly.

"So you think there are about 10 acres of land and it is privately owned by Don Swyndall?"

"Yes."

"Has the property ever been developed before?"

"Not that I know of."

"Well, it is possible that it could be identified as wetlands, but the fellow at the zoning commission was right when he told you about there being ways around that. You can agree to move the wetlands to another location or minimize the impact of the development on the area. And unless there is an endangered species living in James Woods, as a private land owner, Mr. Swyndall doesn't need to be concerned about wildlife. Since it's his private property, he doesn't have to make it a wildlife refuge unless he wants to." He pauses for a moment, and Marcie can feel disappointment descending on her shoulders like a blanket. "The petition idea is a good one if people really feel strongly and are willing to be vocal about it. Does that seem to be the case?"

"I think people would be opposed to it, but not enough to actively do anything about it. My parents don't like the idea of developing the woods, but because Mr. Swyndall is president of the university, they feel like they can't really do anything. Even my grandparents seem resigned to it, but I don't think he should be able to spoil our lake just because he has more money. Isn't there anything we can do?" A hint of desperation creeps into her voice.

"Now, don't lose hope," he says kindly. "We've beaten tougher situations than this before. The problem for my organization is that the land is privately owned and a relatively small parcel. Here's our strategy for now—I'll get our people to look into the wetlands issue. Tell Eric to keep working on the petition, and you should also alert the local newspaper about what is going on. Although they might see the development in a positive light, at least it will bring it to the public's attention. The Cultural Resources angle would really be our best strategy, but since nothing has been found there up to now, it doesn't seem likely. Why don't you get back to me . . . " she hears the rustle of pages turning, "early next week. I'll be out of town until then, and that will give us time to see if these strategies are working."

"Okay," Marcie says faintly.

"Hang in there. It's not over yet. If something comes up between now and then, call Sara's mom and she'll know how to get in touch with me."

"Thank you. I really appreciate your help."

"No guarantees, but we'll see what we can do."

Marcie replaces the receiver on the phone and looks out the window above the kitchen sink at the darkening sky over the cove. Even though Mr. Clements didn't offer her any new ideas, she still feels hopeful. *Maybe there is a way to stop the development,* she thinks, *there has to be a way.*

ca Fourteen ca

MARCIE PARKS HER bike in front of Kaitlyn's house, takes off her backpack and drops it to the ground. This morning when she woke up, she almost wished that it was raining so they wouldn't have sailing practice. She feels a little awkward about being at the Swyndalls' house now that they are trying to stop the development of James Woods. At least no one knows anything about what she and Eric and Al are doing, but they will after Eric gets the petition going and contacts the newspaper that morning.

Sighing, she stretches her arms over her head. The ride over on her bike is only about two miles along the road in front of the lake cottages. It passes James Woods, and Marcie was a little relieved when she didn't feel anything unusual as she pedaled past the cool dimness of the shade beneath the trees. She grasps the loop handle on the top of her backpack and walks up the front porch stairs. Reaching for the brass knocker on the front door, she raps a few times. Almost immediately, the door swings open and she is greeted by Kaitlyn wearing a bright pink sports bikini.

"Great! I was waiting for you," Kaitlyn says. Marcie had called before she left to make sure sailing practice was still on. "Kyle and Conner are out on the boat. We've got a cooler of soft drinks and some snacks." They pass through the entryway and into the kitchen. "Do you need to change?" Kaitlyn says, eyeing Marcie's shorts and t-shirt. "You can use the back bathroom."

"These are swimming shorts and I can just take off my t-shirt and stuff it in my backpack," Marcie says as she peels her shirt over her head to reveal her tank-style suit. There is no way she is going to run around on the boat with her rear end hanging out of her bathing suit.

"Suit yourself—get it? I just crack myself up some-times. Let's go. Bring your stuff on the boat. Maybe we can stop at the Yacht Club for lunch and swim in the pool if Kyle and Conner want to go."

On the dock, Mrs. Swyndall is sunbathing in one of the lounge chairs.

"Ready for sailing? I'm so glad this is working out for you two. It'll be fun to race in the Regatta!" Mrs. Swyndall has a wide-brimmed hat on to shade her face, and several magazines on the table next to her. "Kait, your dad called earlier to say that he has to stay at the office the rest of the week. At least he can come back this weekend." She gets up to adjust her lounge chair. "Have fun." *So, she won't have to see Mr. Swyndall again until this weekend*, thinks Marcie. Not realizing that she had been holding her breath, she lets out a little sigh of relief.

They walk down to the end of the pier where Kyle and Conner are checking the lines, sails, and equipment to get the boat ready to sail. They're both wearing swim trunks and t-shirts. Kyle's sunglasses are fastened to a strap that loops behind his head to keep them from getting lost if they fall off while he's out on the water. They look up as the girls approach.

"What do you think of our new racing scow? We have a cabin cruiser from when we lived back east for the ocean, but the Yacht Club here races scows," says Kaitlyn.

"It's really nice," says Marcie. She knows from hanging around Eric and the Boat Company crowd that it is a top-of-the-line, high-performance racer. Scows are dinghy-style sailboats, like her sunfish, without a cabin and much longer, with more sails and rigging. Racing scows are built for speed.

"Why don't we start by sorting out crew responsibilities. I'll be helmsman and handle the tiller," says Kyle, asserting himself as the captain right away. "Conner, you want to handle the main sail?"

"Sounds good," replies Conner. He adjusts the rim of his faded, blue baseball cap to better shield his eyes from the sun.

"Kaitlyn, you can manage the jib sheet and the centerboard." Glancing at Marcie, he tilts his head to the side and says, "I hear you're a pretty good sailor—can you handle the spinnaker and watch the telltales?"

"No problem," says Marcie, thankful that it's true. Her grandparents' schooner isn't the right type of boat to compete in the Regatta, but it has a jib and a spinnaker, and Marcie has spent many happy hours every summer sailing it with her family. She's very comfortable around most sailboats. Now she is content to follow Kyle's lead.

"Great. Now I know this goes without saying, but I just want to be clear since this is our first time sailing as a team." Kyle counts off each item on his fingers. "Each crew member needs to watch for boat traffic and wind direction." They all nod. "Also, we all need to be aware of weight balancing on the boat and change position as needed." More nods from Kaitlyn, Marcie, and Conner. "This is basic stuff, but I don't want anyone feeling like they have to wait to be told. We all know what to do, so Just Do It!" he concludes with a laugh.

"Yeah!" says Conner.

"We're ready!" says Kaitlyn. As she and Marcie climb aboard to take their positions on the boat, it rocks gently beneath them. They are all wearing flat, rubber-soled deck shoes so they can keep their footing on the slippery, moving boat. Marcie moves to the front of the cockpit to be near the spinnaker and stows her backpack under the foredeck with the cooler. On race day they won't bring any additional stuff with them, as it might get in the way. Kaitlyn sits across from her to handle the jib with Conner beside her. Kyle is next to Marcie with the tiller in hand.

"Everyone ready?" Getting agreement all around, he says, "Hoist the sails!"

Conner starts hauling on the main line, or halyard, pulling hand over hand, and the main sheet rises up the mast. Kaitlyn raises the jib, which is the sail in the front of the boat attached at the prow by a line that connects to the top of the mast. There is a mild to moderate wind today and both sails begin to fill with wind. Marcie doesn't raise the spinnaker, as it is only used when sailing downwind—the same direction as the wind is blowing—to catch additional wind. Kyle steers the boat with the tiller, and they move out past the buoys and into James Bay.

A sailboat sails most efficiently when upright, and the wind is constantly pushing against the sails and tilting the boat sideways. The centerboard projects below the hull and counteracts the push of the wind against the sails. Kaitlyn will move the centerboard up and down as needed to adjust for the wind. Balancing the weight of the crew in the boat in relation to the push of the wind is a very important part of sailing, and you will often see crew members leaning way out over the side of the boat with their feet under the toe lines in the cockpit to counter balance the force of the wind.

They pass a Mennonite family fishing on a pontoon boat as they exit the bay. Conner says, "I didn't think Amish people were allowed to use motors. They are so weird. Beards and goofy hats and the women in their bonnets, like pioneers! No TV, computers, cell phones—like the stone age!" He's leaning back laconically against the side of the boat.

"No shopping at the mall, either," says Kaitlyn. "You wouldn't catch me dead in one of those outfits."

"I'm sure none of them would be caught dead in one of these outfits," says Conner, referring to Kaitlyn's bathing suit.

"I'm sure you're right," Kaitlyn laughs and tosses her loose hair over her shoulder flirtatiously.

Marcie thinks of Rachel and her family at the market. "They must be Mennonites," she says. "I think Mennonites can use motors and electricity, but I don't know about TV's."

"I'm with you—too weird for me," says Kyle. "I can't even imagine living up here all year round. It's a great place for the summer, but there is nothing else going on except the lake. What do people do for fun around here, watch the corn grow? I did see a sign for drag racing on Saturday night, but can you imagine the crowd that would go to that? A lot of rednecks, I bet." They are out in the lake now, having cleared the mouth of the bay. "Why don't we do a couple of easy runs across the lake and back past the sandbar to get used to crewing together? Then on Thursday we can work on speed."

They take a starboard tack upwind towards the sandbar. Marcie watches the telltales on the mainsail for optimal wind position while the others are working the sails. They are sailing easily, getting a feel for each other and the boat. She doesn't meet anyone else's eye when she says, "My family likes coming up here during the off season. It's slower-paced than back home, but that's what we like about it. The lake is really nice then, too, without the summer crowds."

"I did notice there are a lot fewer boats out during the week than on the weekends. Good for sailing, but I would die of boredom living up here all year round," says Kaitlyn.

The wind has picked up now that they are out on the main lake, so they concentrate on sailing. Marcie keeps her eyes on the telltales, letting the others know how the wind is flowing over the sails so they can adjust as necessary.

"See that fishing boat ahead?" says Kyle not waiting for an answer. "We'll use that as our marker to turn back downwind for the second leg of the 'race.' Marcie, you know what to do with the spinnaker." It is a statement, not a question.

"All set," says Marcie. She readies herself for action.

They approach the fishing boat from the port side and wait for the optimum moment to come about without losing speed. Marcie climbs onto the foredeck and attaches the spinnaker pole to the mast and the sail in readiness for hoisting the sail. Her heart is pounding with excitement. Kyle is in charge now, watching the sails and saying "wait, not yet . . . just a little farther." Just as they are about to lose the wind, Kyle yells "Come about!" The others spring into action, quickly switching the direction of the sails. As the boom swings across the boat, Conner calls out "Boom!" They all duck. Marcie is poised to act when she gets the signal from Kyle. He steers them around the fishing boat and as they begin to head downwind, he calls out, "Spinnaker!" Marcie raises the sail. It unfurls in a beautiful cloud of robin's egg blue. Immediately it fills with wind, and they are off in the other direction.

"Perfect turn!" calls out Kyle. "We've got a great chance at beating the rest of the field if we keep working together like that." They do high fives all around. Marcie is as pumped up as the others about winning the race.

Sailing downwind always feels strange to Marcie. It's almost as if there is no wind at all because it's blowing in the same direction as she is sailing, so she doesn't feel it moving past her. The boat hardly seems to move at all, even if she is going fairly fast. Not like when she is sailing upwind and she can feel the wind blowing past as she sails through it.

They do two more practice runs and congratulate themselves on working together so well as a team. Kyle expertly docks the boat at the Yacht Club pier, and they tie off. Many of the other boats docked are racing scows as well.

"It looks like this will be our major competition for the July 4th Regatta," says Conner, indicating the other boats. "But I don't see too many that can compare with our boat, Kyle. We've got the crew and the boat to win," he says with confidence. The two boys are walking ahead of Marcie and Kaitlyn on the dock on their way to the boathouse.

"I'm pretty sure only the Boat Company will be racing a new high performance scow. And I can't imagine that the Townies will have anything that can compete with us. We're in good shape."

Marcie cringes inwardly at the word Townie. Even though most of the Yacht Club members are summer people, many of the club employees are locals with summer jobs, and Kyle is definitely saying it in a derogatory way.

The Yacht Club is part country club and part sailing club. There is a formal dining room where parties are held, an informal dining room, and an outdoor pool. Because they are wearing their bathing suits, they have to eat at the cabana by the pool. Kaitlyn is totally unconcerned about walking around in only her bathing suit, but Marcie is glad to be wearing her shorts.

Tables are arranged poolside in front of the thatched roof cabana. They choose a table under an umbrella, and a waitress pulls herself away from her conversation with the bartender to take their order. Mostly burgers and salads are served outside. They place their orders, and Kaitlyn signs for the meal saying, "It's great not to have to carry any money here—especially since I don't have pockets!" She smiles and glances at Conner.

They spend an enjoyable afternoon swimming and relaxing by the pool. Everything they could want is provided for them—towels, sunscreen, soft drinks, and snacks are all available from the cabana. *I could get used to this life*, thinks Marcie. It seems like it's free, but she knows it comes at a price, and it all goes on Mr. Swyndall's bill. The house, the sailboat, the Yacht Club—everything. She feels a twinge of guilt about using his hospitality while trying to fight the James Woods development, but only a twinge. As the waitress sets another drink down next to her chair, she turns her head away and slathers on more sunscreen.

∝ Fifteen ∝

"I DIDN'T HAVE too much luck with the petition, but the newspaper was interested," says Eric. They are sitting in the rocking chairs on Al's porch after dinner. Al glides gently back and forth on the swing, and Pansy is curled up on her cushion in the corner. "I actually did some work today while you were off sailing and lounging at the Yacht Club," he says testily to Marcie.

Annoyed at Eric for honing in on her conflicted feelings about her relationship with the Swyndalls, she retorts, "I was practicing for the Regatta, as you well know. You're just worried that our team will beat the Boat Company team. And besides, if I hadn't been over there on Sunday, we wouldn't know about the development at all. Consider me a spy for our camp."

"We're not worried," he replies, but he is only somewhat mollified, and adds, "Still, you were having fun while I was going door to door with the petition. Most people were sympathetic and signed, but nobody felt strongly enough to help us take a stand against Swyndall and the developers. It was really depressing how resigned everyone is to letting him tear down James Woods and build luxury vacation homes." He glances over at Al, who so far hasn't said anything, but is listening intently. "The worst was old Marge Appleton who asked me to change the light bulb in her pier lamp post, and after I had done it she forgot that she had asked me and kept asking me to do it again. We went round and round with that for a good five minutes, and she never could understand about the petition or the development." He sighs, leans forward in the chair with his elbows balanced on his knees and rests his chin in his hands. "Maybe the newspaper article will get public opinion against it."

"What happened to the gung-ho crusader of yesterday?" asks Al. The rays of the setting sun glint off his reading glasses as he gestures with the pencil he'd been using to do the crossword puzzle. "It's too soon to give up. Marcie's got Mr. Clements working on it, and the newspaper article will definitely create a stir. People around here may be slow to action—but get them riled up and who knows what could happen? There may be other forces at work around here that we can't control."

"I'm glad you're confident," says Eric, "because the newspaper reporter is going to call you for an interview to get the local residents' point of view after he gets the details from the zoning department."

"I would hope that my opinion will carry some weight with the community. I've lived here all my life and know just about everyone in town and on the lake."

"I think it's our only hope," says Eric, burying his chin in the palms of his hands.

WEDNESDAY MORNING IS rainy and gloomy. A steady drizzle soaks the grass and Mamaw's flower beds—*she'll be happy about that*, thinks Marcie—and low-hanging clouds turn the sky and lake a dull gray. Marcie has taken a book to the loft and is cozily ensconced on the window seat surrounded by pillows and snuggled under a quilt. She likes days like this when you can hang around not doing anything in particular. The rain has a calming effect on the world, and the repetitive sound it makes on the roof of the sunroom below is reassuring. As much as she enjoys the outdoors, sunny days can make you feel pressure to go out and do something fun and exciting. It's nice to have a break. The phone rings downstairs, and a few minutes later Mamaw calls up. "Marcie, it's your mom on the phone. Hurry, she can't talk for too long."

Marcie is reluctant to leave her quilt cocoon even though she's wanted to talk to her mom for days, but she runs down the stairs to the kitchen phone.

"Hi, Mom!"

"How are you, hon? I've missed you and the boys." Her mom sounds just the same even 2,000 miles away.

"I'm good. I miss you, too." She hesitates. "I've been practicing with Kaitlyn for the Regatta. How's the dig going?"

"We're getting ready to go back out right now. Its only 8 a.m. here. The students are doing well, and we're finding some great stuff. I still can't believe this site—an untouched example of western cave dwellers. It was on this rancher's property all these years. He knew about it, but didn't tell anyone until after his death when he left instructions in his will to give the land to the University of Utah. Amazing." Marcie can hear the excitement in her mom's voice. "What about you? Any luck stopping the development?"

"We're working on it with Al. Eric's doing a petition, and he got the newspaper interested. They're going to run a story in this Saturday's edition with an interview of Al against the development. I even called Mr. Clements to see if he could help. I'm not sure if he can do anything, though."

"I'm sorry Marce. I wish there was something I could do to help."

"Well . . . " Marcie wonders if she should tell her. Part of her wants to tell someone about all these things that are happening, but part of her isn't ready to talk about it. *Don't tell her. There's nothing to it. She has enough to worry about at the dig.*

"What is it, honey?"

"I guess I'm just discouraged. It doesn't seem like we're getting anywhere."

"Maybe one of the things you've got going will work."

Eric and Drew come into the kitchen wet from the rain and dripping water onto the tile floor.

"I want to talk to mom now." Drew reaches for the phone.

"Hang on a minute. Let me say goodbye." Marcie swivels away from his grasp. "The boys are here, I have to go."

"Bye hon. Keep trying—you never know what can happen."

❧ Sixteen ❧

When Lucy arrives with Michael and Jayne to spend the afternoon at the cottage, the sun is burning off the last remaining clouds from the morning's showers.

"It looks like we're going to have a nice afternoon, thank goodness. Fishing and swimming in the rain isn't very fun," Lucy says while unbuckling Jayne's car seat and handing her over to Marcie.

"Hello, baby," coos Marcie and gives Jayne a big kiss.

"Not baby, big girl." Jayne pats herself on the chest.

"Yes, a very big girl!" laughs Marcie. "You're heavy!" She sets Jayne down on the driveway. "Why don't you be a big girl and walk, and I'll hold your hand." To Lucy she says, "Mamaw has set up the wading pool in the yard, and Poppy has the fishing poles out by the dock. Eric and Drew are already down there. Do you want me to change Jayne into her suit?"

"That would be great," Lucy replies. "I still need to get the rest of the paraphernalia out of the car—including Michael!" She gives Marcie a flowered bag with clothing in it. "Her suit's in there somewhere."

"Okay. Let's go swimming, Jayne." Marcie leads the toddler into the house.

Jayne is too little to swim in the lake without an adult, so they have a wading pool and water toys for her to play with. Marcie plays tea party with Jayne, and they serve everyone "tea" with water from the pool. Then Jayne wants to water the flower garden, which entertains her for quite a while. She doesn't do much actual swimming in the pool, but her vivid imagination provides plenty of ideas for play. When Jayne wants to play mermaids with her Barbies, Marcie decides she's had enough. The boys have already tired of fishing and are swimming in the cove, leaving Poppy to fish by himself. Marcie wants to get back to the book she was reading this morning and the empty hammock beckons her. She goes onto the porch to get her book and a pillow, passing Mamaw and Lucy on her way.

"I'm going to read in the hammock for a bit, so I won't be watching Jayne."

"That's fine," says Lucy. "Thanks for playing with her. I really appreciate the break." She and Mamaw are sitting in the shade of the maple tree in lawn chairs. A few minutes earlier Al and Pansy had joined them and the three of them lined up in a row look like a panel of officials judging an event.

"While you're up, would you bring out the pitcher of iced tea in the fridge and four plastic glasses?" calls Mamaw. "Relaxing is thirsty work."

"Sure." Marcie gets the drinks and a soda for herself and puts everything on a tray to carry it out. She places the tray on the low table by the chairs and pours out drinks for the adults. The fourth drink is for Poppy, so she carries it to him at the dock.

"You're a sweetheart," he says to her as he takes a long drink.

"How're they biting?" Marcie asks.

"Not bad—see for yourself," he says, pointing to the fish basket that hangs over the edge of the dock into the water. As Marcie leans over and pulls it up, water cascades through the mesh sides and bottom to reveal five large blue gills and one croppy.

"These all look like keepers to me!" she says. She knows he must be pleased.

"They'll do—I've even thrown several back. Eric and Drew gave up too soon. Do you want to join me?"

"It's tempting, but I'm going to read in the hammock for a while." She crosses the yard to the little rise where the hammock is suspended between two oak trees. The angle of the trees allows her to see the yard and the wading pool and down to the dock and the slide where the three boys are playing. She gets the hammock swinging gently with her foot on the ground and then lets it rock slowly to a halt before pushing off again. After a while she glances down and sees Jayne standing on the grass a few yards from the pool playing with Pansy. Jayne is laughing because every time she tries to walk forward toward the lake Pansy gently blocks her. Marcie smiles to herself, but doesn't think much about it and goes back to her reading. She assumes the adults are paying attention.

A few minutes later, she hears Pansy barking and Jayne crying, and she sits up to see what is going on. Jayne is much closer to the water than before, but she is sitting on the ground bawling and Pansy is standing between her and the water barking very loudly.

Marcie has had several dogs as pets, so she knows that they have different barks to mean different things. This bark was not your friendly "hello" bark or an angry bark for the delivery man, but an insistent "something is wrong" bark. Lucy jumps up from her chair and rushes over to Jayne saying, "No Pansy! You're scaring Jayne. Bad dog!" Pansy stops barking and crouches to the ground with her head down and her tail between her legs in a submissive pose.

Marcie runs down the hill "Wait!" she calls out. "I saw the whole thing. Jayne was trying to get around Pansy to get to the water. Pansy tried to block her, but couldn't so she barked to get our attention." She stops to catch her breath. "Pansy saved her from falling into the lake!"

"Oh!" Lucy exclaims. "I guess we were a little engrossed in our conversation. I didn't notice that Jayne had gotten out of the pool until I heard Pansy barking. Come here, girl," she calls to Pansy. "It's okay. I'm sorry." She hugs Pansy with one arm and Jayne with the other as Pansy licks both of their faces and wags her tail enthusiastically. "You saved my baby! But how did she know?" Lucy looks enquiringly at Al and Mamaw, and at Marcie, who is also kneeling beside Pansy and stroking her head

"I don't know, but she was definitely blocking her from going down to the water. Jayne was laughing—she thought it was a game. I assumed you were all watching and knew what was going on. I'm sorry."

"No need to be sorry, we should have been watching," says Mamaw. "Thank goodness Pansy was there. We always knew she was special."

"She is very aware of how I am feeling." Al clears his throat and adds: "It's comforting to have her hovering around me when I'm not feeling well."

"I'm just glad she was watching out for Jayne. You're a good dog." Lucy hugs Pansy more tightly and is rewarded with another swipe of pink tongue on her cheek. She stands up and lifts Jayne onto her hip. "After all that excitement I think it's time for Jayne to have a nap!" She goes into the house, and that seems to be the cue for everyone else to disperse to their own activities. Mamaw gets her gardening shears to deadhead flowers in the garden. Marcie goes back to the hammock to finish her book, and Al ambles over to watch the boys swim…

AL SITS IN one of a pair of Adirondack chairs positioned on the lawn to appreciate the best view of the bay. Al has lived his entire life on the lake and has seen a lot of changes during those 80 years. The cottages have grown bigger over the years, and the boats are bigger and more powerful. All the water recreation gear; the skis, wake boards, water trampolines, inner tubes for three, four, five or even more people, is more complicated and technical. *Back in my day we had a raft and our swim trunks, or a pail of worms and a bamboo pole,* he thinks. Not that it's all bad or that he wishes for the old days—far from it. He loves the Internet and uses his computer to look up the weather conditions for fishing and to shop online. It's so much easier than going into the city. And he wouldn't trade his Zebco fishing pole for anything. Watching Eric and Drew playing swamp monster with Michael, jumping off the diving board, laughing and splashing each other, he knows that the essential things haven't changed much. Kids and families enjoying themselves and spending time together. The extra trappings are certainly nice, but they aren't really necessary to enjoy the lake and its beauty.

He doses off in the chair for a few minutes and then wakes with a start when Eric lets out a yell as he jumps off the diving board into the dark green water. The older Al gets, the more his dreams include family and friends who are no longer living. Sometimes they seem as real to him as the people who are still alive. He thinks it may be because he is getting closer to the end of his life, so he is more attuned to it. It is comforting to visit old friends and loved ones in his dreams.

"Al, look at my jump!" Drew calls out to him. "It's a sea slug!" Al obliges by watching Drew leap from the board and land in a belly flop with a tremendous splash. He claps appreciatively when Drew resurfaces. Al feels lucky to have such a good relationship with the Horton family. Spending time with the children really adds joy to his life.

"What should I do for this dive?" Drew calls to Al.

Al cups his hands to his mouth and yells, "How about a starfish?" Drew jumps from the board with his arms and legs spread wide and a big smile on his face. Al can't help but smile, too.

✑ Seventeen ✑

AFTER SAILING PRACTICE on Thursday, Kaitlyn and her mom planned to go shopping, but Marcie didn't feel like tagging along. She finished her book yesterday and wanted to go to the library to check out a new book. She thought sailing practice had gone really well that morning. The four of them are experienced sailors and know what to do in their respective jobs on the boat. It's more a matter of learning to work together as a team and anticipating what needs to be done and what the others are doing at any given moment so the whole process goes smoothly. Marcie feels confident in her abilities as a sailor and in her role manning the spinnaker and keeping track of the wind flow. Since she didn't feel any nervousness, she was able to relax and feel the joy of sailing. She never gets tired of the wind in her hair, the movement of the boat on the water, and the exhilaration of feeling propelled through the waves by the wind.

They did several runs up and down the lake working on speed and timing, and Kyle was especially pleased with their performance. "Great work everyone," he said several times. "I feel really good about how we're progressing as a team. What do you think about racing in this Sunday's Regatta?"

"It would be good practice, and we could take a look at some of the competition," Conner answered. "But would we be tipping our hand by racing before the 4th?"

"Maybe you're right."

"I don't know if that will really matter," Marcie shrugged. "The Sunday Regattas go on all summer long. People with lake houses aren't here every weekend, and full-time residents don't race every Sunday. According to Eric, it's a different race every weekend because the participants are always different. The Boat Company team might be out racing though."

"That could be a good thing—we'd see how we stack up. Let's think about it. We don't have to decide right now," Kyle said as they brought the boat in to dock and set about stowing the sails and halyards.

Now, as she rides her bike along the main road into town, Marcie decides not to tell Eric that they might race in Sunday's Regatta. She knows he's been practicing with the Boat Company team this week too, and she doesn't want them to race on Sunday just to compete with her team. If they race, fine, she just doesn't want to push the issue.

She glances up at the canopy of leaves overhead. This is one of her favorite streets. All along the parkway on both sides of the road, enormous ash trees grow. Their branches arch out over the street to meet in the middle, forming a tunnel of green as high as a cathedral. To Marcie, it seems like a king or queen should be riding horseback majestically down the center of the boulevard.

The library is in a red brick building one block off Main Street. The original library was in a converted Georgian-style house with white pillars and a veranda, but a modern brick and glass annex was added several years ago. The combination isn't as strange as it sounds, but Marcie thinks it looks a little bit like the library sprouted wings off its backside where the addition flares out to surround a glass-enclosed atrium. It's a bigger library than you might think a town of this size would need, but the summer crowd uses it often too. Marcie is glad, because it means they almost always have the currently popular books available. She loves the library and usually checks out more books than she could possibly read before the due date.

Walking up the sweeping staircase and through the front door, she takes the first right into the young adult section. They have a number of books displayed on a table in the center of the room surrounded by comfy couches for reading. She stops at the table to peruse the books, as they are probably newer releases that she hasn't read yet. A few seem interesting, so she reads the jacket cover and inside flap, and selects three to check out.

After checking out her books at the circulation desk, she passes a large map of Lake Pappakeechee and the surrounding area on the wall. She stops to look at it more closely and sees that it has the locations of Native American sites in the area as well as the trading routes used by Native Americans when they lived here. Lake Pappakeechee isn't the only lake in the region, but it is the largest. There are many smaller lakes, and most of them are connected by rivers and marshes. Most of the sites on the map are from the Miami tribe, but there is one that is noted as an Adena site, located on the shore of the largest river in the area. It is almost at the edge of the map. It shows an area with three circles in a line. A dotted line is drawn down the centers of the circles, connecting them, and there are dotted lines bisecting the centers of each circle in diagonal directions. She hadn't even thought about looking anything up about Native American sites—until now. Something about the Adena circles makes her think. Turning around, she approaches the librarian at the Reference Desk.

"Excuse me, do you have any books about the Adena Indians from this area?" Marcie asks the librarian. She notices that her name tag says MISS ROBINSON.

"Let me see." She lifts the glasses hanging on a beaded chain around her neck and places them on the bridge of her nose before turning to her computer. "Is that spelled A-D-E-N-A?" She types rapidly on the keyboard.

Marcie nods and answers, "Yes."

The librarian peers more closely at the computer screen. "It looks like we do have a small section with the other books on local history." Miss Robinson turns her gaze to Marcie again. "We also have a small display case with items found by locals—mostly arrowheads and pottery shards and the like. I'm not sure that any would be Adena, though. I'll show you the books and where the display case is located." Marcie follows her over to the stacks. "The books should be in this section." Miss Robinson indicates a section on the second shelf of one of the stacks. "And the display case is down at the end of the non-fiction section in the atrium. Let me know if you need anything else." Her skirt flares out as she turns and walks briskly back to the reference desk.

Marcie looks at the titles of the books and sees that only three are relevant, so she brings them all to the table at the end of the shelves. Taking off her backpack, she places it against the table leg. The first book she selects is titled *Mysteries of the Adena People*. She opens the book and sees an artist's drawing of a circular mound of earth with Native American people sitting on the mound facing a man standing at one end with his arms in the air. He must be a chief or priest, judging by his more elaborate dress. Marcie can hardly believe her eyes. The picture is strikingly similar to the vision she had in James Woods. With shaking hands, she turns the page and begins skimming the first chapter. It says, the Adena Indians, or "Mound Builders," were named after the farm in Ohio where the first site was discovered. The farmer called the property Adena, which is a Hebrew word meaning "beautiful land." They are identified with mounds they built out of earth. The mounds were aligned with the rising and setting points of astrological bodies and were often used for ceremonial purposes. The ceremonial mounds are sometimes called "sacred circles" by archaeologists. On the next page is a list of more than 50 astrological alignments that one of the mounds studied by archaeologists was found to predict. The right hand side of the page has a drawing similar to the one on the map on the library wall—three circles in a line bisected by dotted lines. The dotted lines show how the mounds are aligned with celestial activity. *Just like Stonehenge*, Marcie thinks. The Summer Solstice Sunrise and Moonrise, the Equinox Sunrise and Moonrise, and the movements of many other stars, planets, and constellations are on the list. She doesn't even know when the Equinox is during the year, and these people kept track of it by building a mound of earth! The book also says the mounds are often found near rivers or bodies of water. That fits with what she saw too. The mound had been on the shore of a lake, maybe Lake Pappakeechee. But Bob at the zoning office said there aren't any Native American sites on the lake. Sacred circles and celestial bodies . . . Marcie shivers, but not from the air conditioning.

Closing the book, she gets up from the table, and walks past the non-fiction section and down a ramp to the atrium. The two-story space is open on three sides to the library stacks. She looks for the display table and sees it positioned next to the low wall surrounding the atrium. Sunlight streams in from the glass wall at the far end of the room and reflects off the glass top of the case.

The artifacts are arranged on beige felt under the glass with labels showing where they were found. She's surprised to see that a lot of arrowheads and pottery shards were found in James Woods. Then her eye is drawn to something in the corner of the case . . . a copper bracelet. Her breath catches in her throat. An image from her memory of the dark-haired girl wearing a copper bracelet flashes through her mind. The label says it was found in James Woods. She grips the sides of the table to steady herself.

The wooden side of the table feels loose in her hand. Looking down, Marcie sees that it is hinged on the bottom like a door. She pushes against the wood and it folds open, revealing the artifacts inside. Someone must have forgotten to lock it. The bracelet is resting right at the edge of the felt. She could easily touch it. Her hands are sweating now, and she wipes them on her shorts. She quickly looks around and sees that no one is watching her. Tentatively, she reaches for the bracelet. Her fingers touch the cool metal and . . . nothing happens. She had been expecting something, like an electric shock, to surge through her. She slips the bracelet on her wrist. It feels cool against her skin. Its hammered surface sparkles in the sunlight. She removes the bracelet from her wrist and begins replacing it in the case, but at the last minute shoves it in the pocket of her shorts. Luckily, no one is nearby in the atrium to see her take it. She closes the side door on the case. She doesn't really think about what she's doing—that she's actually stealing the bracelet. She quickly gathers up her books and checks out, mumbling replies to the librarian's questions. She gets on her bike and rides home, her mind in a whirl.

IT ISN'T UNTIL later that night, after dinner, that Marcie allows herself to really think about the copper bracelet. Sitting on the window seat in the loft, she looks out at the night sky. The maple tree partially obscures her view, but she can see the stars winking in and out behind the leaves fluttering in the breeze. The bracelet is still in her backpack where she put it when she got back from the library. Marcie walks over to her bunk and retrieves it. She turns it over in her hands and then places it on her upper arm like the Indian girl wore it. She regards her reflection in the full-length mirror on the bathroom door. Was it a mistake to take it? She's never stolen something before, and it's giving her an uncomfortable feeling. What can the bracelet really tell her about the Native Americans anyway? As she is pondering this thought, she notices her image in the mirror begin to blur, and then, slowly, the room around her starts to fade away.

At first everything is dark, but she can tell she is outside. Gradually, as her eyes adjust to the darkness, she can make out her surroundings. Several fires are burning and she is kneeling with many other people in a circle. Her hands are resting in her lap on a leather tunic and the skin on her arms and legs is light brown. Around her arm is the copper bracelet. She has the strange feeling that she is looking through the eyes of the Native American girl and can sense her thoughts and feelings, but that she herself is still separate. The sky is absolutely covered with stars. Marcie has never seen so many stars before.

She realizes that she is sitting on a mound and notices that there are wooden poles set at intervals around the perimeter of the mound. The girl seems to be waiting in excited anticipation for something that is about to happen.

Everyone is chanting quietly together and then at a signal from the man who the girl thinks of as the Holy Man, they all fall silent. Their attention is drawn toward one side of the mound where two poles are connected across the top with another pole. As they all watch, the full moon appears over the horizon perfectly centered between the two poles. As it rises, it becomes a huge orange globe suspended in the blackness of the sky, surrounded by brilliant stars. It's a breathtaking sight. Marcie recognizes it as the harvest moon that rises in the fall. The gathered people let out a collective sound of joy, and the Holy Man begins chanting again. She senses the event has significance for these people for the changing of the season, the bounty of the harvest, and preparation for the winter ahead. It is a time for celebration.

She is so deep in the image that she doesn't hear Eric coming up the stairs.

"What're you doing?" he asks as he reaches the top of the stairs.

Startled back to the present, Marcie jumps and her heart starts pounding wildly. "Uh . . . nothing," she says too quickly. Reflexively, she grabs the bracelet off her arm and starts to put it behind her back, but Eric snatches it from her and says, "What's this?"

"Oh, it's just a bracelet that . . . ah, Kaitlyn gave me." She stutters and tries to grab the bracelet from him.

He holds the bracelet in the air just out of Marcie's reach. "Sooo, why don't you want me to see it and why are you acting so funny? Are you embarrassed to be accepting gifts from Kaitlyn?"

"I'm not acting funny, you just startled me, that's all. I'm not sure that I'm going to keep it anyway. But I'm not embarrassed."

Eric rubs the surface of the bracelet before tossing it back to her. "Whatever. It's nothing special anyway." He walks over to his side of the room, opens the drawer beneath his bunk and pulls out a sweatshirt. "Poppy is taking us night fishing if you want to go. We're leaving in ten minutes."

"Yeah, I'll go. I'll be down in a few minutes."

Eric swings around the newel post and down the stairs. Marcie sits down on her bunk and lets out a huge sigh. *That was so dumb! Why did I act that way and call attention to the bracelet?* He had taken her by surprise as she was seeing the tribal ceremony. The bracelet definitely has a connection with the people in her visions. She gets down on the floor and shoves the bracelet under the mattress at the foot of her bed. Her sweatshirt is hanging on a peg on the wall. She grabs it and goes downstairs to join the others.

❧ Eighteen ❧

AT BREAKFAST SATURDAY morning, all the talk is about the article in the paper on the Swyndall development and the interview with Al.

"I think the tone of the article is definitely in our favor," Eric says, tapping his knife on the edge of his plate. "It says, *The nature park, as it was initially promoted, is only a small part of what will eventually become an exclusive community of estate homes.* The reporter doesn't actually say that Swyndall lied, but does imply that the entire truth wasn't told." Eric pauses to take a bite of toast. "Al, your interview is great!" He uses his piece of toast as a pointer to indicate Al, who is standing on the patio outside the sunroom with Pansy. Aloud, he reads, "*Local resident Al Depena says it would be a shame to develop one of the few remaining wild and marshy areas of Lake Pappakeechee. He also says, 'I've lived here all my life and seen generations of residents use James Woods for recreation. The James family always welcomed use of the woods by all the lake residents. I'd hate to see it used exclusively for a privileged few.'* That's right on target, Al. Hopefully it will get people to fight the project!"

"I just told them what I thought about the development. We'll see whether it makes any difference."

"They even mention the petition I'm taking around. Maybe I'll go out again this afternoon and show people the article. It might get them to sign the petition and get more involved," Eric says while buttering another piece of toast.

Mr. Horton arrived at the cottage the night before and is enjoying his coffee and newspaper on the porch. Looking at Marcie and Eric over the top of his reading glasses, he says, "I hope it doesn't have too much of an impact. I have a tee time with Don Swyndall at 9:30. It'll be pretty uncomfortable if he's angry about what you kids are doing. Making enemies with the Swyndalls wouldn't be great for my career. You might recall, he *is* the president of the university."

"The kids are doing a good thing. It's nothing more than the truth," says Mamaw, as she stirs cream into her coffee. "People have a right to know what Swyndall is up to, even if it won't stop the development. Money and power usually seem to get their own way."

"That may be true, but it doesn't have to be a bad thing," says Marcie, pushing her hair behind her ears. "Look at Sara's family. They have gobs of money, but they use it to do good things for our town. They donate money to all sorts of causes, and her dad works for an environmental watchdog group. Money is just money. It's what you do with it that matters."

"You're right, Marcie. And don't be too quick to judge the Swyndalls," says Mr. Horton, folding his newspaper to the next page. "I happen to know that they are generous philanthropists, and Mr. Swyndall is president of a public university that provides higher education to thousands of students. Mrs. Swyndall is very active in the University Foundation, which is involved in many good causes."

"It's easier to believe they are bad guys for developing James Woods if I don't know about those things. I guess it's more complicated than that."

"Yes, it is. Sara's father may be doing a lot of good works with his money now, but he inherited it from his grandfather, and some people say his fortune was made in some less than respectable business deals."

"I didn't know that," Marcie says quietly.

The ringing of the phone interrupts their conversation. Marcie jumps up to answer it. Coming back to the table, she says, "That was Kaitlyn. She wants me to go water skiing with her this morning. She didn't say anything about the article, so maybe it isn't a big deal. Dad, could you drop me off at their house?"

"Sure. We'd better get going soon if I'm going to make my tee time."

"SO, I SEE you and your brother have been busy this week!" Mr. Swyndall claps Marcie on the shoulder. She and her Dad are standing in the entryway of the Swyndalls' house.

"Oh, uh . . . yeah," Marcie says hesitantly. She's pretty sure he's referring to the article about the development, but she doesn't want to get into a discussion about it. She's glad her dad is there.

"I saw the article in today's paper."

Mr. Horton quickly jumps in. "You know how kids can be, Don. They're just sad to see James Woods go. They've played there for years. They may have gotten a little over-zealous."

"Oh, I totally understand. In fact, I respect them for it. The thing is, the new community represents economic development for the area, with new jobs and services. It's progress. You'll see." He wags his finger in the air. "It's a good thing for the area. We're still planning a nature trail and a bike path for people to enjoy." He pauses, rubs his hands together, and looks from Marcie to her Dad. "Anyway, it's a done deal. All the permits and approvals are in place. Now that everyone is aware of the estate home portion of the project, we can move ahead with that more quickly."

That's great, Marcie thinks. Now the development will happen faster! At least he's not acting really mad. That would have been awful, especially for her dad.

"Well, we're glad you're not taking it personally, Don. They really meant no harm. I have to say, I'll miss the woods myself. But I understand progress." Marcie feels a little bit like her dad is selling out to Mr. Swyndall by making light of the whole thing. But then, what choice does he really have?

KAITLYN SIGNALS THAT she's had enough after skiing two loops of the south end of the lake, let's go of the rope, and sinks slowly into the water. Marcie calls out, "She's down!" to Kyle. He slows down and turns the boat around to pick up Kaitlyn.

"Do you want to go next?" he asks Marcie, turning in the driver's seat to look at her.

"Sure. I think I'll use the kneeboard though."

Kyle has turned out to be a pretty nice guy, Marcie thinks, as she pulls the kneeboard from the side of the boat. At least when he's not being snobby about the Townies and the Regatta. She goes to the back of the boat to help Kaitlyn. "Hand me up the ski," she says. "I'm going to use the kneeboard. You were great out there!"

"Thanks. The water is just right—not too wavy. It's a good thing we came out early, before the other boats make it too choppy." She hands Marcie the ski and pulls down the stairs at the back of the boat. Marcie stows the ski in the side of the boat, and Kaitlyn climbs aboard dripping water onto the floor. Sitting on the back of the boat, Marcie fastens her life jacket and climbs down the ladder into the water. Kaitlyn hands her the knee board and raises up the ladder. Marcie likes the kneeboard and has mastered a few tricks and turns on it. As the name implies, you kneel on the board with a strap across your thighs. She's also a very good skier, but it's fun to try something different. She hasn't tried wakeboarding yet, which is somewhat similar to snowboarding, where you stand on a board with your feet fastened into boots. You can do jumps and turns and even flips. Maybe next summer for that . . .

In the water she bobs up and down with the waves as she sorts out the rope and gets situated on the board. She signals that she is ready to go, and Kyle starts to accelerate. You start on the kneeboard lying on your stomach and then pull yourself up after you get up to speed. Once she is kneeling on the board, she fastens the strap over her thighs. She can go in and out of the wake pretty easily, but the most fun is spinning around on the board. It helps to wear ski gloves so you don't tear up your hands on the rope—the kind that don't have fingers. First Marcie pulls the rope handle into her chest and holds it with one hand. Then she turns in the opposite direction from that hand with her knees, pulling the rope handle close into her back and literally skiing backwards, with her hand holding the rope behind her back. She grabs the handle with her other hand, lets go with the first hand, and finishes the turn so that she is facing forward again. It all happens very fast, and if you are good you can turn circles one way and then another or spin really quickly in one direction. Marcie hasn't gotten quite that good yet. One or two turns is about all she can do.

When Marcie returns to the boat, Kyle brings up the Sunday Regatta. "I don't think we should race in the Regatta this weekend. We don't want to tip our hand to the competition too soon. We all have enough racing experience that I'm not concerned about our first real race together being the 4th Regatta. What do you guys think?" They all agree that it will be fine to skip the race on Sunday, although Marcie doesn't know why it would matter. Lots of people race in weekend regattas. She thinks winning the race may be a little more important to the others than it is to her.

Conner goes out next on the slalom ski. Kaitlyn and Marcie are sitting together in the front of the boat, but they are still spotters for Conner. Kaitlyn says, "We saw the article in the paper this morning about my dad's development in James Woods."

"You did?" Marcie says in a small voice. She had been waiting to see if Kaitlyn would mention it.

"We didn't even know he was planning to build houses there. He always has some kind of deal he's working on."

"Was he mad about the article?" Maybe he was just acting like he wasn't mad with her and her dad.

"No, he just laughed about it. He says there's always someone who wants to try and stop progress. Why do you want to stop him from developing James Woods? It's just trees and reeds. My dad says they're going to keep part of it as a walking and biking trail."

"It's our special place. It's one of the last natural parts of the shoreline left." Marcie finds it hard to express to Kaitlyn exactly why they're opposed to the development. "James Woods has always been there, even before my grandfather was a kid. It just doesn't seem like we need any more luxury homes on the lake." Even to Marcie's ears, it sounds kind of lame. She doesn't want to say that building really expensive homes makes the lake more exclusive and unavailable to anyone but wealthy people. The

Swyndalls are just the kind of people who could buy those homes.

"I can see why you might feel that way, but, I mean, it's just trees. Dad says there isn't anything that can be done. He has all the permits. It's all approved and perfectly legal." Kaitlyn stretches her legs out across the seat in the bow of the boat and leans her head back to catch the rays of the sun. With her eyes closed, she says, "I wouldn't put out too much effort trying to stop it. My dad usually gets what he wants."

That's just what Marcie is afraid of.

THAT NIGHT ON Al's porch, she tells Eric and Al about what happened at the Swyndalls. Eric agrees with Marcie that their dad should have done more. "You'd think he could at least say something to try and convince Swyndall not to develop the woods." He bangs his hand on the arm of his chair. "I only got two phone calls from people who were interested in signing the petition. They didn't want to get more involved than that. It's pretty discouraging." He pushes his hand up through his hair and leans back heavily.

"Maybe we should just accept that there is nothing we can do about it," Marcie says resignedly.

"I'm not ready to give up yet," says Al. "We can't see now what to do, but we may still find a way. We just have to take the next obvious step and see where that gets us. It's like driving in the dark with your headlights on. You can only see 200 feet in front of you, but you can travel all the way across the country that way—200 feet at a time."

"That sounds great, Al, but we're not driving a car, and I can't see what the next obvious step is," says Eric. "Something needs to happen soon or the development is going to move ahead."

⊗ Nineteen ⊗

MARCIE OFFERS TO take Drew and Michael on a walk. Her dad left to go home shortly after lunch, but Aunt Lucy and the kids are staying for dinner. Actually, only Marcie walks. Drew and Michael ride bikes from the selection of kid's bikes that Mamaw and Poppy keep on hand in the garage. Drew can ride a two-wheeler, but Michael rides a tricycle. Marcie wants to go to James Woods, but she doesn't really want to go there alone. Having the little boys there with her seems like it would make it less disconcerting. On their way out, they pass Al coming out of his house to take Pansy on a walk.

"Mind if I join you?" he asks. "I need to get a little exercise."

"Sure, we're going to the woods."

"Well, I think I can make it there if we don't go too fast."

They walk in companionable silence while the boys ride a short way ahead on the path that runs along the road. They fall farther behind as Pansy has to stop and sniff the bushes repeatedly along the way. Marcie doesn't want the boys to get too far ahead, but she also doesn't want to rush Al. She calls out, "Drew, Michael, wait for us at the edge of the woods!"

"Okay!" they shout back.

Marcie realizes that she hasn't thought about Al's health since Monday and feels bad that she didn't think to ask him about it. He never complains, so she assumes that everything is fine. "How are you feeling?" she asks.

"I can't complain. Some days are better than others, and today's a good day. On good days I try to go a little farther on my walks with Pansy. I've got to keep up my stamina and keep an eye on what's going on in the neighborhood. It might fall apart without me, you know," he says with a smile.

When they reach the edge of the woods, the two boys are waiting. They get off their bikes and Drew says, "We're going to play Indian tracker and leave our bikes here. Come on, Michael!"

"Just stay where we can see you. We don't want any of those Indians to get you!" Marcie says with a laugh. Since she is just joking, she is taken aback when Michael says in all seriousness, "Don't worry, they won't bother us. They're friendly." He turns and runs after Drew. "Wait for me!"

"He said that like there really are Indians in the woods. He has a vivid imagination, doesn't he? The other day he told me he could fly."

Al doesn't answer her right away. Just then, Pansy sees a squirrel and starts barking and trying to run after it. Marcie has been holding the leash for Al, so she is distracted with holding the dog under control. When the dog settles down, Marcie says, "Lately, I feel like I'm the one with the vivid imagination. Really strange things have been happening to me."

"What sort of things?"

"Well, twice I've sort of imagined that I was flying. I had a flying dream where I flew over the lake to James Woods. It was kind of creepy, but it was just a dream. It's not like I think I can fly or anything." She says this dismissively, but her laugh is forced.

There is a rustic bench beside the path at this point, and Al sits down on it. "Let's rest here while the boys play." They can see Drew and Michael darting behind trees and bushes farther down the path. Marcie gazes up at the leaves overhead. She is really going to miss these woods. They are so peaceful and beautiful. She's seen deer and even a fox in the woods over the years, in addition to the usual birds and chipmunks and squirrels. Where will these animals go when the houses are built?

"I'm no expert on dreams," Al continues. "I believe we use our dreams to sort out things that happen during the day. Maybe you were just worrying about James Woods."

"I'm sure that's it," Marcie replies, but she's not sure about much of anything lately. Neither of them says anything more for a few minutes. Marcie can feel the copper bracelet in her pocket digging into her leg. She brought it with her to the woods to see if she could re-create what happened in the loft, but she's afraid to try. *What if something really does happen? What do I do then?* She pulls it out from her pocket and lets it rest in her lap. It feels warm and seems to glow a little in the dappled shade of the woods, like it has a brightness all its own. Al looks over and sees the bracelet in her lap. "Where'd you get that?"

"Oh, I . . . ah, found it in the woods last time I was here." *Why did I say that? At least I should keep my story straight.*

"Let me see." He reaches over and picks up the bracelet. Marcie is half-hoping, half-afraid that something will happen when he touches it. He turns it over in his hands, examining it. "Interesting. It could be an artifact. You can ask your mom about it when she gets home." He hands it back to her, and Marcie immediately puts it back in her pocket.

"I don't think it could be old. Someone must have dropped it accidentally."

"Maybe. But there's something about the design that makes me think it's older. Maybe primitive. You don't see that kind of decoration these days."

Marcie hadn't paid much attention to the designs etched into the bracelet, but now she pulls it out of her pocket to look more closely. She sees that there is a carving on the outside of the bracelet of three circles connected by a line with the moon at one end and the sun on the other end. It reminds her of the mounds and how they track the movement of the sun and moon. The carving looks like it was done by hand. Realizing that she is holding the bracelet and nothing is happening, she thinks about putting it on her arm, but something is holding her back. It feels warm and tingly in her hands, but that's all. She doesn't put it on. The scene before her eyes stays just the same. Marcie calls Drew and Michael back for the walk home.

"How was your game of Indian Tracker?"

"It was fun," Michael says, "but the Indians had to leave, so we played Forest Ranger instead."

"They had to leave, did they?" asks Al as he ruffles Michael's hair. "Where did they go?"

"Back to their own time."

"Well, of course," says Al with a smile at Marcie, as if to say 'isn't he something else?' Marcie smiles back, but inside she's wondering what Michael really does see.

At the edge of the woods, the boys pick up their bicycles and pedal ahead. Marcie looks at the bracelet. It no longer feels warm to her touch, it is just cold, hard metal.

❧ Twenty ❧

THE PHONE IS ringing Monday morning when Marcie and Mamaw come in through the back door with bags of groceries. Marcie deposits her bags on the counter and picks up the receiver.

"May I speak to Marcie Horton, please."

"This is Marcie."

"This is Miss Robinson, from the library." Marcie feels her throat tighten. "I helped you last week when you were looking for books on the Adena Indians." Eric comes into the kitchen and is looking through the bags for something to eat.

"Oh yes, I remember." Marcie's voice comes out squeaky through her clenched throat. Mamaw returns to the kitchen with more bags of groceries. She gently smacks Eric's hand away from a box of cookies. "If you want something to eat, you need to help put the groceries away first."

"I'm calling because we're missing a bracelet from the Native American Artifact display case, and you were the last person I remember being interested in it." After a short pause, she says, "I got your name from the Adena books you checked out."

"Really, a bracelet is missing?" squeaks Marcie. Eric quickly glances her way. Marcie turns her back to him.

"Yes, I wondered if it was in the case when you were here—or if you knew anything about it?"

"No, I don't remember seeing a bracelet."

"Really, so it was already missing when you saw the display case?"

"I guess so, 'cause it wasn't there when I saw the artifacts." The lie comes easily to Marcie.

"Well, it was worth a try. Sometimes people 'borrow' things from the library and return them later. Just like our books." She is giving Marcie a way of saving face if she has taken the bracelet.

"Oh, really? Well, sorry I couldn't be more helpful. I hope you find the bracelet, or it gets returned." Hanging up the receiver, Marcie turns around to find Eric standing directly behind her, listening.

"Who was that?" he asks.

"Oh, just someone from the library." Marcie tries to move past him, but he blocks her way.

"It sounded like they were missing a bracelet—could it be the bracelet you had the other night?" He is speaking softly, and Mamaw is across the room, so it is unlikely she can overhear their conversation.

"Yes, they are missing a bracelet, but not the bracelet you saw the other night. I told you, Kaitlyn gave that to me." Marcie can't look him in the eye.

"I don't believe you." He is a few inches taller than Marcie and is glowering down at her now. "You were acting funny about it the other night, and you're acting guilty now. Did you take it?"

"I told you, I didn't!"

"Well, I'm not going to say anything, but I think you should return it," he says, as Marcie slides past him towards where Mamaw is putting away the groceries.

"Yeah, whatever," she says, but she is thinking that she will return the bracelet as soon as she can figure out how to do it without getting noticed. Maybe she could just put it in the book return slot . . . but then it might get damaged. She takes a gallon of milk off the counter and puts it in the fridge. She could try to slide it back into the case without being noticed . . .

"I mean it," says Eric, eying Marcie over the top of a grocery bag as he takes out cans of soup.

"What are you kids arguing about," asks Mamaw.

"Nothing," they both answer.

❧   ❧   ❧

THAT EVENING, MARCIE calls Mr. Clements to see if he has been able to come up with anything to help stop the development. Marcie can't help but think of how his grandfather may have made his fortune doing something illegal. It changes how she thinks about Sara and her family. They definitely use their money and power for good purposes, but Marcie doesn't think of them as being so perfect anymore.

Mr. Clements isn't very encouraging. "I'm sorry to say, there doesn't seem to be much we can do to help. The land is private property, and Swyndall has all his permits in place. With our limited resources, we have to choose our battles, and since it's such a small parcel of land, it doesn't look like it's a fight we're willing to take on," Mr. Clements says apologetically. "It's too bad, because the land has never been developed and represents a lake shore ecosystem. Did you have any luck getting public opinion against the project?"

"Not really. Eric got a petition going, and the paper ran a story. Most people weren't in favor of the project, but they weren't strongly opposed to it either. Definitely not enough to rally against it."

"Well, at least you can say that you tried," he says with a note of resignation in his voice.

"Yeah, I guess so. Thanks anyway." Marcie can't help feeling that Mr. Clements has let her down. She had placed so much hope in his ability to help.

"I'm just sorry we can't do anything." As she replaces the receiver, Marcie feels like she's closing the door on the last hope for saving James Woods.

❦ Twenty-One ❦

MARCIE'S ALARM SOUNDS shrilly in her ear, and she reaches over to turn it off.

7 o'clock. Race day. She swings her feet onto the floor and stretches her arms over her head. Sunlight is streaming through the window onto the floor. Good. With luck there'll be a strong breeze, too.

She looks across the room at Eric in his bunk. Her alarm must have roused him from sleep too, as she can see him stirring.

Marcie gets clothes and her bathing suit from the drawer under her bed and pads barefoot to the bathroom to change and get ready. She regards her reflection in the mirror. *I really want to win today*, she thinks. She enjoys sailing for the sheer fun of it, but there seems to be more at stake for her with this race. The others want to win, too, but perhaps for different reasons. Marcie feels like she has something to prove—but to whom? To herself? The Swyndalls? Or maybe to Eric? She's not really sure. She brushes her hair, pulls it behind her head and secures it into a ponytail. When she emerges from the bathroom, Eric is also up and dressed. He's sitting on his bunk, putting on his shoes, his hair still messy from sleep. They both need to meet up with the rest of their crews and get out on water. The race begins at 10 o'clock.

"I guess I'll see you out on the water—as we leave you in our wake, that is," Eric says mockingly.

"Don't be so sure."

"Why? Will you be wearing your bracelet for luck? 'Cause you'll need it."

Marcie ignores this remark and gets her shoes from the closet. The bracelet is under her mattress. She hasn't looked at it all week. It annoys her that Eric knows about the bracelet, but she's not about to show it.

"I'm going down for breakfast," he calls over his shoulder as he descends the stairs. "See you at the finish line!"

Eric's comment about the bracelet starts her thinking. She retrieves it from under the bed and puts it on her upper arm. The sleeve of her t-shirt comes down to her elbow and covers the bracelet. *Maybe I will* wear it for luck, she thinks. She quickly puts on her shoes and follows Eric down the stairs.

When Marcie joins Kaitlyn, Kyle, and Conner at the dock, there is an air of quiet anticipation among the group that draws Marcie in. They are too excited and perhaps a little too anxious for small talk, so they work silently on the task of getting the boat ready for the race, lost in their own thoughts. The mainsail and the jib are ready to hoist, and the ropes are coiled on the deck. "Marcie—check the spinnaker and then we should be ready to go," Kyle instructs her.

The spinnaker is stowed in a bag at the front of the boat. Marcie climbs onto the foredeck and checks that everything is in order. "All set," she calls out as she scrambles back to her spot in the cockpit.

"Okay. Let's paddle out from the dock," Kyle says, as Kaitlyn unties the ropes. Conner and Marcie paddle the boat out into the bay. Marcie feels a shiver of excitement run through her when they hoist the sails and they fill with wind.

For the start of the race the boats don't simply line up and start sailing from a standstill. The starter will sound a ten-minute warning, and all the crews will maneuver their boats in an attempt to sail across the starting line just as the starting gun goes off—but without crossing the line too soon. If you cross the line early, you have to take a penalty—circle back and start again. You want to cross the line in full sail to get the best start to the race. It's tricky to time it exactly right, especially as there are 20 other boats all trying to do the same thing.

Kyle is busy giving instructions. "Marcie, since we won't be using the spinnaker until the second leg of the race, you can watch for boats and call out the right of way." Marcie will need to be very alert. There are some fairly complicated right-of-way rules involving leeward and windward positioning and starboard and port tack. Hitting another boat when you don't have the right of way is a foul that results in a penalty.

Conner checks his watch. "There's still plenty of time to get to the starting line. Let's warm up for the race and get a feel for the wind conditions."

Marcie says, "Eric was acting pretty cocky this morning, talking trash about beating us. I'd love to beat him and rub his face in it."

"Yeah, I saw some of them at Smokey's Landing the other day, and they were gloating about how this year's win will make five in a row. As though it was already a done deal," Kyle says as he steers the boat out of the bay.

"Those Townies are too confident for their own good. We'll see what they have to say when we beat them," Conner says. He adjusts the mainsail to catch the wind.

They practice a few turns in the bay and then begin sailing toward the starting line, an imaginary line between the starter's boat and a marker buoy. They are still a good distance away from the start when the ten-minute warning horn sounds.

"We're in perfect position," says Kyle. "Outside the pack with a little more distance to cover, but not as much boat traffic." He takes his sunglasses off and lets them hang from the lanyard around his neck. "We need to sail toward the line and time it for the starting horn." They take a port tack with the wind blowing over the left side of the boat.

Marcie notices that the Boat Company crew seems to have the same idea and is slightly behind them on the side closer to the starter's boat. The race is beginning before they even reach the starting line, as the two boats jockey for position.

Conner is timing their approach to the start and adjusting their speed with the mainsail. "Two minutes to go," he calls out. Marcie's heart is pounding and her mouth is dry. She looks over at Kaitlyn manning the jib sail and catches her eye. Kaitlyn's expression of intense concentration turns into a broad smile, and she gives Marcie a thumbs up with her free hand.

"One minute." Conner starts calling out ten-second intervals as they are fast approaching the marker buoy. Almost at the same instant that the starter's horn sounds… they cross the starting line. They've timed it perfectly. They let out a collective cheer. It seems to Marcie as if she'd been holding her breath for ages.

"Full out!" shouts Kyle, and they're off. They got a jump on the whole field, including the Boat Company, and they want to capitalize on the lead to stay in front.

"Boat approaching on the starboard side. Between us and the Boat Company," Marcie alerts the team. Another boat, with a red stripe along its hull, is not far behind them, between their own boat and the Boat Company. Looking under the sail, Marcie can see Eric manning the jib sail of his craft and the rest of his crew balanced on the port side to counteract the force of the wind. Marcie has moved over next to Kaitlyn and Conner to do the same thing, but she's still keeping a careful eye out for other boats.

"We'll continue on a port tack," Kyle yells over the wind.

Marcie is watching the tell-tails, and she calls out, "We're losing wind speed. Turn more to port." Kyle and Conner adjust the direction with the main sail and the tiller. The key now is to keep ahead of the pack and stay on the windward side of the other boats to keep the wind in their sails.

They will travel in a zig-zag pattern down the course. They want to come at the buoy from a close starboard tack so they can swing around the buoy and not lose time by making too wide a turn. Timing will be critical.

"Ready to come about—on my mark," Kyle calls out. "Three . . . two . . . one—now!" Kyle steers them left with the tiller, Conner and Kaitlyn pull the lines of the sails to the opposite side of the boat, and everyone moves to switch sides. Marcie ducks as the boom swings across.

"Crap! Our timing was off on that one," exclaims Conner. "We lost our momentum and didn't catch the wind right away."

"We don't want to give those other two boats any opportunity to catch up," says Kaitlyn.

"The red stripe boat is upwind of us now," Kyle says. "They could block some of our wind if they move ahead."

Red stripe and the Boat Company also come about to switch directions. The Swyndalls' boat is just barely in the lead, but that could change at any time. A couple of other boats further down the line aren't far behind either.

Now that they are facing the other direction, Marcie can see all the spectators in speed boats anchored far outside the race course. For a quick instant she looks for her family, but can't place them in the crowd. She looks behind her and sees that the Boat Company has caught up with them. From just a few yards across the choppy water, Eric is looking right at her with a wide grin on his face, as if to say 'it's not over yet.'

"The Boat Company has right of way for the next turn," she calls out. "Keep it tight or we could have a problem clearing them."

To get maximum speed, they are all leaning out over the side with their feet under the toe-lines to counteract the force of the wind in the sail and balance the boat. Water is splashing up over the sides as the boat slices through the waves. They complete the next turn successfully, but the red stripe boat has edged ahead into the lead. After two more turns, they are approaching the halfway buoy and have a slight lead over the Boat Company team.

"Get the spinnaker ready," Kyle shouts to Marcie over the sound of the wind and waves. She is already climbing onto the foredeck to attach the spinnaker to the mast. On the unprotected foredeck she has to deal with the rocking movement of the boat and the water coming up over the deck as it dips into the oncoming waves. She will need to raise the spinnaker after they swing around the buoy. "Prepare to come about!" calls Kyle. "Marcie, on my mark."

She sees the official race boat anchored out from the marker buoy to monitor the competitors as they pass.

As they are approaching the buoy, Marcie hears a dog barking. But she doesn't see any dogs.

It must be on one of the spectators' boats. Then she realizes that she knows that bark—it's Pansy barking. A loud, insistent bark—coming from the direction of James Bay. How can that be? She looks for Al's boat among the spectators, but doesn't see it. Somehow, Marcie knows that something is terribly wrong and Pansy is barking for help. Her bark is like an alarm sounding in Marcie's brain,

communicating the need for action. She has to get to Al…
now.

Without thinking about what she's doing, Marcie dives
off the sailboat and starts swimming. A Department of
Natural Resources boat is anchored next to the official's
boat. Marcie recognizes the DNR man on the boat; she
thinks his name is Brad. She's met him before out on the
lake fishing with Al. She is in open water and swimming
rapidly towards the DNR boat. Because the Swyndalls'
boat is in the lead and coming around the buoy on the
outside, there are no other sailboats between her and the
boat. Kaitlyn, Kyle, and Conner are yelling at her, but
Marcie doesn't hear them. All she can hear is Pansy's insistent barking. She is only concerned about getting to Al. All
thoughts of the race have flown from her head.

When she reaches the DNR boat, Brad has the ladder
down for her to climb aboard.

"What's going on?" he asks, obviously surprised to see
her jump ship in the middle of the race and swim for his
boat.

"It's Al, Al Depena. Something's wrong. He might be
hurt. He's in James Bay," she says, gasping for breath. The
urgency in her voice and the certainty of her tone must
convince Brad that something is indeed wrong, and he is
galvanized to action.

He starts the engine. "Pull up the anchor." He reverses away from the race and then speeds off in the direction of James Bay. "There's a towel under the bench seat in front," he calls out over the noise of the splashing water and the roar of the engine.

Marcie gets a towel and wraps it around herself. She sits in the front of the boat, watching for James Bay to come into view. They round the point and there is Al's boat at the far end of the bay, in the shallow area by the shore.

"There he is!"

"I see him," says Brad. "Hey—how did you know something was wrong? Did he call you on his cell phone?"

"No, I heard his dog barking, and I knew something was wrong." As she says it, Marcie realizes how improbable it is. How could she have heard Pansy barking from so far away? But she *had* heard it; she still hears it, the insistent barking sounds like 'Help! Help! Help!' to her ears. "Don't you hear it now?"

"Are you kidding? I can hardly hear anything over the engine noise." He looks at her quizzically, but doesn't say any more.

They approach the boat and Marcie can see Al slumped over in the stern. Pansy is standing next to him protectively and wags her tail as they come alongside the boat. Brad kills the engine, and now they can both clearly hear Pansy barking.

"Throw the anchor out. I'm going aboard," he says as he climbs over the side of the speed boat and into Al's fishing boat. Carefully, he checks Al's pulse and breathing. "He's alive, but his pulse is very weak. Hand me the handset from the dashboard and dial 911. I'm calling for an ambulance." Marcie quickly grabs the handset and dials the number. "Is he going to be okay?" She's frightened by the grayish tint of Al's skin.

"I'm going to pull his boat up to the shore so the paramedics don't have to wade into the water." He pulls in Al's anchor, then jumps into the water, which is over his head, and slowly pulls the boat to the shore.

Marcie wants to be near Al and Pansy, so she lowers the ladder and climbs down, intending to swim to shore. She is surprised when her foot touches the sandy bottom and the water is barely up to her waist. As her other foot sinks into the sand, the scene around her starts to blur. She rubs her eyes, but instead of clearing up, the edges of everything become more indistinct, as if she is wearing someone else's glasses. Slowly, a second image begins to come into focus. Like two negatives on the same piece of film, she can see the boats and Brad on the shore with Al and at the same time she can see another image emerging, superimposed over the first. It's almost as if she's in two places at once. Perhaps she is in two times at once. Both images are of James Bay, but in one she sees a mound curving around to form a circle of raised earth. It is empty of people except for one—the girl with the copper bracelet is standing a few yards away, her arms spread wide.

The scene with the girl is becoming more solid, and the image of Al and Brad appears now only transparently over it. Marcie looks down and sees that she is standing on the mound in the past and in the present it is covered with water glimmering under her gaze. She realizes that the ancient mound is actually located *in* the lake in the present time. That's why no one has ever found it! It's been covered by the shallow water of James Bay. Marcie brings her eyes back up to look at the girl and smiles broadly. Could this be what the girl has been trying to tell her? Perhaps there is a sacred site in James Woods, but the shore of the lake wasn't always in the same place.

Marcie and the Native American girl gaze at each other for a moment. Then, Marcie pushes up the sleeve of her shirt to show that she is wearing the bracelet. The girl smiles at her, and then her image begins to waiver and become fainter. The past slowly fades away. Marcie doesn't have time to consider what her discovery means. The reality of the present hits her as she half-wades, half-swims to the shore to help Al. Brad has Al reclining in the boat, but hasn't moved him otherwise.

"His pulse is still very weak. He's lucky you knew something was wrong. It could have been some time before anyone noticed him back here in the shallows."

Marcie doesn't reply. Sirens blare in the distance. She hugs Pansy and strokes her fur. Somehow Pansy got the message to her. She smoothes Al's hair across his brow. His eyes open briefly.

"Hey, kiddo," he says hoarsely, before his eyelids flutter closed again.

❧ Twenty-Two ❧

THE PARAMEDICS ARRIVE and take over. Marcie hears the sound of a speed boat approaching and looks up to see her family arriving in the bay. Her mom and dad swim to shore, leaving her grandparents and Drew in the boat.

"We saw you jump off the sail boat. What happened?"

"Pansy called me," Marcie says to her mom. "I heard her barking, and I just knew something was wrong." Her mom puts her arm around Marcie's shoulders.

The paramedics have Al on a stretcher and are loading him into the ambulance. "Can I ride with him to the hospital?" Marcie's dad asks the paramedics. They wave him into the ambulance as they hook Al up to various monitors. "I'll call you when I know anything," her father says to Marcie and her mom as he climbs in. The paramedics close the door and take off with the sirens blaring, lights flashing, and tires churning up the sandy soil.

Mrs. Horton turns to Brad. "Thanks for your help."

"No problem. I just hope he's okay." He takes off his hat and wipes his brow. "Hey, what happened in the race? It's probably over by now."

The race! "They must be furious with me. I probably cost them the trophy." She pauses. "Mom—I'm really scared. Al looked so awful."

"I'm worried, too, honey."

Mamaw and Poppy take the speed boat back so that Marcie and her mom can drive Al's fishing boat home. They are standing next to the boat, ready to push it into the water and climb aboard with Pansy, when Marcie says, "Mom, I need to show you something. Something in the water."

"What is it?"

"It's on the bottom of the bay. Swim out with me and I'll show you."

As they wade into the water, Marcie grabs some of the small buoys from Al's boat that fishermen use to mark the location of good fishing sites. Once the water is over their heads, they start swimming. "I think it's over here." Marcie swims to the general area where Brad's boat was anchored, and her mom follows. Marcie treads water, reaching down with her feet past the clinging seaweed for the bottom. The top three feet or so of water is warm from the sun, but below where its rays can penetrate, the water is considerably cooler. It's an odd sensation to have the top half of her body in warm, almost balmy water, and the bottom half gradually getting cooler and cooler until her feet and toes groping for the bottom are in decidedly chilly water. When her feet finally do touch, she calls to her mom. "I found it. Here, where you can stand."

"Is it a sandbar?"

"No, I think it's something else. Like a raised shape or mound on the bottom of the lake." Marcie isn't ready to tell her mom more until she's certain that something really is below the water. Maybe she imagined it all. In some ways that's easier to believe.

"A raised shape?"

"Yes. Will you help me figure out what it is?"

"Okay," Mrs. Horton says, puzzled. "Just tell me what you want me to do."

"Let's start walking along the rise. If we place these buoys as we go, we can get an idea of the shape." She drops a buoy with its weighted rope where they are standing. They start tentatively walking in what seems to be the right direction. It takes a few tries, feeling the bottom with their feet, but they eventually figure it out. It is quiet in the bay. A slight breeze ruffles the cattails and reeds near the shore, and nearby a pair of ducks and five ducklings dive for food, their heads under the water searching for tender plants and their tails sticking up in the air. The only sounds are the birds calling in the trees and the splashing of Marcie and Mrs. Horton in the water. They work together companionably in the peaceful scene, thoroughly engrossed in the task; sometimes taking exploratory steps and probing with their feet and sometimes diving down beneath the murky water to explore the muddy contours of the lake floor with their hands. It is slow going. Their clothes are heavy with water. Marcie is wearing her suit under her clothes, but she doesn't want to stop to remove her shirt and shorts.

"This is really interesting," says Mrs. Horton after they've gone about 50 feet. "It's like a narrow sandbar and it isn't really a straight line, more like a curve or an arc. I think it's starting to turn back here."

"Let's place another marker."

"How did you know this was here?"

"When I stepped out of Brad's boat I was right on top of it."

Their excitement builds as a circular shape begins to emerge. Marcie feels her hope growing that it could actually be real, that all of it really happened. When they complete the circle and are back at the first buoy, they turn and look at the buoys they've placed.

"It is definitely a circle," Marcie's mother says. "Like a circular mound of earth . . . "

"Yes, that's right—a circular mound!" Marcie can hardly believe that there really is a mound under the water. She realizes that all the strange occurrences over the past two weeks were gently guiding her to this moment, this discovery.

"I'd almost say it was man-made," her mom continues. "It's too precise to be just a regular sandbar. It reminds me of a Native American mound. It's the right shape and size, but in the bay?"

"I think it is an ancient mound," Marcie says. "It sounds a little crazy, but when I stepped onto the mound from Brad's boat, I could see it in the present and the past at the same time. In the past, it wasn't covered with water." She hesitates and then rushes on. "I've been having these visions all week about Indians." Now that she's started, the story comes pouring out and she tells her mom everything from the flying dream to taking the bracelet and seeing the girl wearing it. She lifts up her sleeve to reveal the bracelet. "See, here it is." She hands it to her mom. "Do you believe me?"

"Of course I believe you." She takes the bracelet and enfolds Marcie in a soggy hug. "What I can't believe is that you kept all this to yourself. You've had quite an interesting two weeks." Releasing her, she says, "Sometimes when I'm at a dig site, I get a sense that the spirits of the people who inhabited the place and used the artifacts are somehow present. I've never actually seen them, but that doesn't mean it couldn't happen." Mrs. Horton looks closely at the bracelet. "This certainly looks like something the native tribe members would have worn. The Adena people are called the 'mound builders' because of the ceremonial mounds they built."

"I read about them in the library when I found the bracelet. I think it's an Adena mound."

"It could be. So, in your vision, the mound wasn't covered with water?"

Marcie nods.

"We do know that the shore of Lake Pappakeechee has changed over time. It's possible that the shore was further out in James Bay when the Adena lived here." Mrs. Horton turns the bracelet over in her hands and runs her fingertips over the design etched into its surface. Slowly, she turns her gaze to Marcie. "This could be a really important discovery. Most of the Adena mounds have been destroyed or damaged by farming or artifact hunters." She continues with a tremor of excitement in her voice. "It could also have an impact on the development of James Woods."

"Because it's a cultural resource?"

"Yes. An archaeological site becomes the property of the state and is protected."

A smile gradually unfolds on Marcie's face. "You mean Mr. Swyndall wouldn't be able to build on the land?"

"I can't really be sure. The mound is in the water, not the woods. But it definitely opens up that possibility. It's really an extraordinary find. I can't wait to get back and contact some of my colleagues about this."

"You won't tell anyone about the visions, will you? It's a little too . . . unusual to share."

"I'll keep it to myself." They stand together on the mound for a few moments looking at the markers and letting the realization sink in. The family of ducks swims gracefully between the buoys on the smooth surface of the water, making V-shaped ripples that expand and overlap behind them to form an intricate design. Below them, undisturbed for thousands of years and hidden beneath the sparkling water, lies what might be an ancient ceremonial site where people worshipped and celebrated, lived and died. A sudden gust of air sends the leaves of the trees rustling, and makes the hair on the back of Marcie's neck stand up.

"Did you hear that?" asks her mom, breaking the spell that surrounded them. "The trees were whispering to us." She shivers and then shakes herself. "Let's get back home and see if there's any news about Al. And I have a few phone calls to make."

❧ Twenty-Three ❧

When they arrive at the Swyndalls' that night, the party is already in full swing. All the competitors from the regatta and their families have been invited to watch the July 4th fireworks, and there is a crowd of people on the patio. It is starting to get dark, and torches are lit at intervals around the edge of the patio to illuminate the area. Christmas lights are draped across the arbor that covers part of the patio. Marcie's parents stop to talk to some people they know, and Eric goes looking for his friends.

Marcie doesn't want to be here at all. She's had to endure Eric's gloating all afternoon. The Boat Company won the Regatta, and he's been needling her about it the whole day. The red-striped boat came in second, and the Swyndalls' boat came in a disappointing fifth place. Without Marcie to man the spinnaker, they lost the lead at the halfway buoy and were never able to catch up. Marcie isn't sure she can face Kaitlyn, Kyle, and Conner.

Hopefully she can avoid them—especially Kaitlyn—by sticking close to her grandparents and not mingling too much. She looks around and spots Kaitlyn over by the dessert table. "Let's get something to drink first," she says to her grandparents, and they walk toward the bar, which is on the other side of the patio from the desserts. Marcie gets a soda from the bartender, turns away from the bar, and who is standing right in front of her but Mr. Swyndall—the other person she wants to avoid tonight.

"Hello there, young lady. You're the talk of the party," he says, not unkindly. "In all my years of sailing, I've never seen anyone jump off a boat in the middle of a race. Why don't you tell me what happened." He is a big man, tall as well as wide, but not fat. Just big. She has to look up to talk to him. It's intimidating.

Marcie takes a sip of her drink to steady her nerves. She can feel perspiration beading on her forehead. Because she's been working at cross purposes to Mr. Swyndall all summer, she feels uncomfortable and a little afraid of him.

When she speaks, her voice comes out as a croak, and she needs to clear her throat several times. "Our neighbor, Al, had a stroke, and he was all alone in James Bay. He needed help, so I had to go to him."

"How did you know something was wrong?" he asks, puzzled. His eyebrows come together to form a V in his forehead.

"I just," she stops, looks down at her glass, and then meets his gaze directly, "knew."

Mr. Swyndall is silent. Finally, he says, "I believe you really did 'know.' I have to act on hunches all the time in my position, and I've learned to trust my instincts. The most important question is—how is Al?"

"He's doing well now. The paramedics treated him in the ambulance, which really helped. He's still in intensive care, but they think he can be moved in the morning." Marcie is surprised to find herself begin to feel at ease with Mr. Swyndall. She realizes that this is the first time she has really talked to him.

"That is terrific news. I think Kaitlyn needs to hear this. They're pretty angry with a certain someone at the moment." Before Marcie can say anything, he has propelled her over to where Kaitlyn and Kyle are standing. "Look who I found," he says. Kaitlyn gives her a withering look, and Kyle glares at her. "I've just learned the reason for Marcie's big dive from the boat, and I think you need to hear it." He looks at Marcie as if expecting her to tell the tale, but takes pity on her obvious discomfort. "It seems that her friend, Al, had a stroke during the race and was all alone in James Bay. Marcie and the DNR man got there just in time to call the paramedics. They saved his life."

"Really?" Kaitlyn's eyes are wide and unfriendly. "So you didn't just abandon us for spite or something? I honestly thought that maybe you wanted the Boat Company to win all along, and when you didn't call this afternoon to explain, that just confirmed it." A breeze lifts her hair and blows it across her face. She brushes it away.

"That was quite a trick you pulled on us today. We were in the lead and ready to take it all the way! That is, until you abandoned ship," says Kyle.

"I'm sorry I didn't call. I know I let you all down, and I wasn't looking forward to talking to you." The coolness of the glass in her hand helps to calm her. She realizes that she doesn't really care if they're still mad at her. Being Kaitlyn's friend is nice, but not as important as helping Al.

"We were pretty mad at you. But I guess it is only a race," admits Kaitlyn grudgingly, her anger apparently dissipating.

"Yeah," adds Kyle, "maybe we can race in some of the regular Sunday Regattas and show them what we can do."

"I'd like that," says Marcie. *Maybe I don't have to choose between my family and the Swyndalls,* she thinks. *I just need to choose what's right for me.*

"I'll call you," says Kaitlyn, as she and Kyle turn and walk away, leaving her alone with Mr. Swyndall.

Marcie sees her mom approaching them, and she groans inwardly. There had been a lot of debate at the Horton household about whether or not to confront Don Swyndall with the news about the mound in James Bay. Since it was the Fourth of July, Mrs. Horton didn't have much luck contacting her colleagues, but she was able to track down the Archaeology Department Chair on his cell phone at a holiday party. Far from being annoyed at the interruption, he was thrilled to hear of the possible site and said he would order preliminary surveys right away. Marcie's dad was of the opinion that they should wait until after the party to confront Mr. Swyndall, since he is sure to be resistant to changing his development plans. Mrs. Horton let it be known that if she encountered him at the party, she would not hesitate to tell him about the mounds. She seemed more concerned about stopping any construction preparation that might begin on Monday than avoiding a scene at the party.

Seeing her mom now and the look of determination on her face, Marcie knows that they won't be waiting to spring the news on Mr. Swyndall.

"Jill, I've just heard the story of your daughter's heroics this afternoon." He places a hand on Marcie's shoulder. "I'm glad to hear Al is doing okay."

"Yes, fortunately, it looks that way, thanks to Marcie and the paramedics." She lifts her head up to look at him directly. "There is something else I want to talk with you about. I understand that you are planning to develop James Woods."

"Thanks to your children that is now common knowledge," he says with a laugh.

"We made a discovery in the bay that may change your mind. Actually you have Marcie to thank for this as well."

"What sort of discovery?"

Mrs. Horton turns to her daughter. "Marcie, it's your discovery. Why don't you tell him?"

"Well," Marcie says hesitantly. Then, taking a deep breath, she continues more confidently. "There may be an Adena Indian mound located in the bay right off the shoreline of James Woods. I found it this afternoon when we were helping Al. We mapped it out with fishing buoys."

"Yes, Marcie literally stumbled upon it in the water. You should know, I've contacted the Archaeology Department Chair, and he wants to do some surveys right away."

"Hold on a minute. You found a Native American archaeological site in the bay?"

"We can't be sure yet, of course, but we know the shoreline of the lake has changed over the last two millennia. There are certain things about the site that lead me to believe it could be an Adena mound." Mrs. Horton likes to talk with her hands, and the plate of cake and glass of tea she is holding have been hindering her, so she places them on a nearby table. "You see, it isn't technically on your land, and the water is the property of the Indiana Department of Natural Resources, but any development of the land would certainly have an impact on the site." Marcie is watching Mr. Swyndall carefully to judge his reaction to the news. She can't read his expression to tell what he's thinking.

"So the site is in the water, not on my land?" *Oh no,* thinks Marcie, *he's going to fight it.* "This certainly does change things." He pauses, momentarily lost in thought. The conversation of the other partygoers flows all around them. Overhead, the strings of lights sparkle in the night sky. "A find of this magnitude could do a lot for the university. I'm no expert on archaeology. If you say it's an important find, I have to take your word on this."

Marcie realizes that she is staring with her mouth hanging open, and shuts it immediately. She had expected Mr. Swyndall to completely oppose doing anything with the site. Mrs. Horton is absentmindedly twisting her napkin in her hands. She says, "It could be a very significant find, if it's undisturbed. Think of what it could mean for the Archaeology Department and the university." She uses the napkin to blot perspiration on her neck. Seeing the opportunity to drive their point home, Marcie says, "You may want to delay construction until we find out more."

Mr. Swyndall takes a long swallow from his drink. The music playing in the background is tuned to the radio station that will synchronize its music with the fireworks. They've been playing patriotic songs all evening. Right now the station is playing a marching band song with cymbals crashing and drums beating. It's almost like a drum roll is accompanying Mr. Swyndall as he contemplates his decision. Finally, he says, "We probably should wait until the site can be investigated." He gives Marcie a pat on the back. "It looks like you might get your wish after all, young lady."

THE NIGHT IS dark now, and the fireworks will be starting soon. Marcie is standing along the shore at the edge of the Swyndalls' property, where she can see James Bay and the deeper darkness of James Woods. The water laps gently at her bare feet, and she feels a profound sense of peace. She likes the feeling of being alone with the party going on distantly behind her. Lights from houses on the shore of the lake shine in the darkness like a string of luminescent pearls, but no lights shine through the trees of James Woods. Now, there may never be any houses built there. Nothing has been decided yet, but Marcie feels in her soul that the woods will be protected. She hugs herself to ward off the chill of the night air, and her hand touches the bracelet on her arm. She will have to return it to the library, but tonight she wanted to wear it one more time. The memory of the girl who once wore it long ago is in the air, but that's all it is—a memory. The woods are quiet now.

The symphonic music on the radio starts to build in intensity, and Marcie hears the shrill whistle of the first of the fireworks whizzing into the sky. The rocket explodes at the same time the music reaches its crescendo and its red, white, and blue light illuminates the sky and the bay and woods below. For a few moments, the trees and the water glow in the patriotic colors and then darkness returns. Marcie turns and walks over to join her family on their blanket spread on the lawn. She squeezes in between her dad and Drew. The next rocket explodes brightly white above them. She looks over at the faces of her family, lit up by the display. Each one of them looks the same as always to Marcie, but she feels different, somehow better. She finally feels comfortable just being herself. She lies back on the blanket to watch the rest of the fireworks, with her family close by her side.

❧ Twenty-Four ❧

THE THICK CARPET of red and gold leaves crunches under their feet as Marcie and Al make their way along the path. Pansy, released from her leash, bounds ahead in pursuit of a squirrel or a rabbit, leaping past the shafts of sunlight that stream through the vibrantly colored leaves on the trees.

"What a great day," Marcie says. "I don't even need this jacket." She shrugs her shoulders out of her jeans jacket.

"Yes, it's Indian Summer—warm weather in the fall after the first frost. I'll take this over the cold rain we've been having any day," says Al.

Marcie glances over at him. He is walking with a cane now, but his gait is steady. He isn't completely back to his old self after the stroke, but she can definitely see improvement from when she saw him last at the end of the summer.

"So, what's the surprise?" she asks now. Her family is visiting the cottage for the weekend, and Al asked her to join him on a walk to James Woods.

"You'll find out soon enough. Young people have no patience nowadays," he says grumpily, but Marcie knows he's just teasing her.

Their progress is slow, but they gradually make their way toward the clearing along the shore of the bay where Marcie found Al slumped over in his boat. Marcie has an idea of what Al's surprise is, but she is still unprepared for the sight that awaits her when they round a curve in the path and the shore is laid out before them. Instead of 30 feet of sandy beach and marshy shallows, the shore stretches out before them for more than 100 yards to a curving stone wall that arcs from one side of the shore to the other to hold back the water in the bay. In the center of the arc is a low circular mound of earth.

Marcie comes to a standstill, and her breath catches in her throat. "Wow, it's really here," she whispers.

"Pretty impressive, isn't it? They just finished the wall this week."

But Marcie isn't thinking about the mound itself, she's remembering everything that led up to its discovery. In the months that passed since then, going back to school and seeing her friends, it became harder for her to believe that any of it really happened. Looking at the mound now, however, she vividly remembers seeing the Adena girl with her triumphant smile standing on the mound that day last summer.

"It's amazing. Can we walk out to it?"

"I don't see why not."

They carefully make their way along the path laid out across the still-soggy ground and stop at the metal fence surrounding the mound. Standing here on this beautiful autumn day, Marcie can imagine the ancient people who worshiped in the same spot thousands of years ago. She has a sense of something sacred. It could be the familiar prickling feeling on the back of her neck, or the wind whispering in the dry leaves of the woods. Whatever it is, she knows that the Adena girl is still here too.

"Mom says they will have a team start excavating sections of the mound in the spring. She gets to be in charge of the dig—and she can make sure they do it carefully, without harming the mound." Marcie puts her forearms on the fence and rests her chin on her arms.

"You know," Al says thoughtfully, "it's thanks to you that James Woods was saved from development."

"I just found it; mom and all the archaeologists from the university took over after that. Once they were certain it was an Adena mound, it was pretty easy to convince Mr. Swyndall into establishing it as a park. He got the grant money that built the wall and drained this section of the bay."

"It was pretty incredible that you found it at all. And that you found me in the bay. I often think about that."

He glances over at her. "You never really told me how it happened."

"I can't explain it, but I knew you needed help." She cocks her head to one side and shrugs. "I heard Pansy barking, and it was like she was calling me. Like something was guiding me to the bay. And when I climbed out of the boat, I was standing on the mound."

"I've always thought there was something special about these woods," Al says, looking around him.

She turns and looks into his wise old eyes for a long moment. "Well, I think we can definitely say that you were right."

MARCIE CUTS THE power on the little trolling motor and lets the row boat glide up to the Swyndalls' dock. None of their boats are in the water now. They're all shrink-wrapped and stored for the winter. Since Marcie's grand-parents live here year round, they leave their boats in the water longer, but this morning, after the family took one last boat ride, Poppy drove the pontoon over to the boat-yard to be hauled out and stored. Only the row boat is left, as it can be hauled out by hand and left on the shore be-fore the lake freezes over.

The back door of the house opens and Kaitlyn emerges, hurrying down the path and onto the dock, her sneakers thudding on the wooden planks.

"I'm so glad you're here this weekend!" she exclaims as she climbs in the front of the boat. "My mom's had me working all morning to close up the house for the winter. Let's get out of here before she finds something else for me to do."

"I thought you'd have a service close up for you," Marcie says, as she starts the motor and maneuvers away from the dock.

"My mom's pretty picky about her stuff. She likes to do it herself."

"I can see how she would be that way," Marcie flashes a smirk at Kaitlyn.

"Hey, watch it, it's not like your family's perfect either," replies Kaitlyn.

"That's for sure!" laughs Marcie easily.

"I thought Sara was coming with you this weekend."

"She was, but something came up with her family and she couldn't make it."

"You know, I was thinking that next summer we should have a girls' weekend up here. You can invite Sara and some of your friends, and I'll invite some friends."

Marcie steers the boat in a slow loop around James Bay, past the new retaining wall around the Adena mound.

She gets a warm glow of satisfaction seeing the mound and the woods from the water and knowing they are safe and that she had a part in it. She puts the boat in idle and lets it gently drift with the current.

"That's a great idea." After a moment's hesitation, she adds, "What do you think about getting a team together for the Regatta next summer?"

"Are you sure you want to be on a 'Laker' team?" Kaitlyn asks with a slightly mocking tone. But Marcie can see that her smile is friendly.

"I raced with you all summer, didn't I?"

"Yes, but you also ruined our chance to win the Regatta."

"Are you still mad at me about that?"

"I was totally mad at you when it happened. After all the practicing we did, and we were in the lead when you jumped! We were all really angry and disappointed at the time. But I'm over it. Actually, now I think what you did was awesome. It took guts. And I don't just mean diving off the boat. My dad thinks what you and Eric did about the woods was pretty cool, too."

"He does? But it stopped his project."

"Yeah, I know, but he's funny about that kind of thing. He respects people who 'stick to their convictions.'" Kaitlyn makes quotation marks in the air, then she throws her hands up and sighs. "Let's not talk about my dad all afternoon. It's our last boat ride of the season!"

Marcie turns back and engages the motor. She feels a smile forming at the corners of her mouth. When she jumped off the boat to help Al, she did it instinctively because it was the right thing to do. It didn't matter what anyone else thought. Yet she can't help but be pleased that she has earned Kaitlyn and Mr. Swyndall's respect, too.

As the little boat picks up speed, they leave the Adena mound and the woods behind them. When the boat passes the mouth of the bay, Marcie opens the throttle wide and they skim across the surface of the lake to open water, two girls enjoying the day, hair streaming behind them, the warm sun on their backs, and smiles on their faces.

TRACY RICHARDSON

About the Author

Tracy Richardson wasn't always a writer. When her children started reading and she rediscovered all the books she loved as a child, she found herself developing stories of her own and began writing novels for children.

Images from her childhood growing up on Lake Michigan and the landscape of Indiana feature prominently in her novels, and sometimes bits and pieces of actual people and events—much to her children's delight and dismay! She lives in the suburbs of Indianapolis with her husband and two children and their Jack Russell terrier, Ernie.

Visit Tracy online at www.tracyrichardson.wordpress.com.

Discussion questions for *Indian Summer* are available online at www.luminisbooks.com.